"We have to get him."

"I will." Patrick watched the man tug Jennie's son along toward the truck. "Stay here." Patrick unclipped the leash from his dog, Tucker, and dropped it to the ground. Then he clicked his tongue again.

Tucker moved with him, keeping beside Patrick's leg in a perfect "heel" where he tracked with every footstep Patrick made.

They were partners. Each one watching the other's back.

The gunman shoved Nate toward the truck.

The boy cried out, a sound that rang across the mountainside as clear as the night sky. Patrick took two more steps and brought his gun up just as another man emerged from the house.

"Hey!" Jennie screamed down at the valley. "Hey, I'm right here! Come and get me!"

He nearly faltered.

"Mom!" The boy screamed for her, the sound of it so full of fear that it hurt to hear.

A gunshot rang out, whizzing above Patrick's head. He hit the dirt, and Jennie screamed.

Lisa Phillips is a British-born, tea-drinking, guitar-playing wife and mom of two. She and her husband lead worship together at their local church. Lisa pens high-stakes stories of mayhem and disaster where you can find made-for-each-other love that always ends in a happily-ever-after. She understands that faith is a work in progress more exciting than any story she can dream up. You can find out more about her books at authorlisaphillips.com.

Books by Lisa Phillips

Love Inspired Suspense

Double Agent
Star Witness
Manhunt
Easy Prey
Sudden Recall
Dead End
Colorado Manhunt
"Wilderness Chase"
Desert Rescue

Secret Service Agents

Security Detail
Homefront Defenders
Yuletide Suspect
Witness in Hiding
Defense Breach
Murder Mix-Up

Visit the Author Profile page at Harlequin.com for more titles.

DESERT RESCUE

LISA PHILLIPS

LOVE INSPIRED SUSPENSE
INSPIRATIONAL ROMANCE

LOVE INSPIRED® SUSPENSE
INSPIRATIONAL ROMANCE

ISBN-13: 978-1-335-40494-7

Recycling programs
for this product may
not exist in your area.

Desert Rescue

This edition published by arrangement with Harlequin Books S.A.

For questions and comments about the quality of this book, please contact us at CustomerService@Harlequin.com.

Love Inspired
22 Adelaide St. West, 40th Floor
Toronto, Ontario M5H 4E3, Canada
www.Harlequin.com

Printed in U.S.A.

Behold, I will do a new thing; now it shall spring forth; shall ye not know it? I will even make a way in the wilderness, and rivers in the desert.
–Isaiah 43:19

To all the dog lovers out there, this one's for you.

ONE

"Come on." Jennie Wilson held tight to her son's hand as they crept down the back steps of the house.

A house where they had been held for hours. Nearly a whole day, if she'd correctly tracked the rise and subsequent fall of the sun.

"Run, Nate. Stay right by me."

His smaller hand gripped hers, fingers tight. Nate was nine years old. It had been just the two of them since she'd found out she was pregnant and the father had split town like he didn't care at all. Since her father had died of a heart attack when Nate was two.

Nate and Jennie.

They didn't need anyone else. Or, at least, they hadn't until yesterday, when gunmen took them from their home after dinner and escorted them here. Left in an empty room, not tied up. The door unlocked. They'd sat there all night and then all day while those two men yelled threats and waved guns around.

She was done waiting for rescue that might not even come. She'd seen those two men out the window, standing in front of the house, talking. Jennie had tugged Nate down the stairs to the back door so they could make a run for it.

Nate stumbled. He inhaled sharply, and she stopped to catch him. But he hadn't gone down, just planted one knee in the ground at the bottom of the stairs and launched back up like he hadn't stumbled. She could've hugged him. The kid wanted to get out of here as badly as she did.

Over his shoulder Jennie spotted a man at the back door, looking out. He was a huge, dark figure, silhouetted by the light inside. But she could see the gun in his hand.

"Come on." Her words were a harsh whisper in the dead of the New Mexico desert night.

The house was set into the side of the mountain, hidden from the town's view. Terrain around them was dust and sagebrush. Shrubs. The occasional growth of sand shinnery oak, which was nothing more than a bush.

There was nowhere to go.

God, keep us hidden. She didn't want their escape to be in vain. Only God could hide them from these men.

"Hey!" The gunman's growl rang out.

Jennie tugged on her son's hand, but in his tennis shoes he was faster than her. They raced together down an incline, what amounted to the yard of this abandoned house. Would she rather be dead than a hostage? Now was too late to ask herself that. The damage was done.

She'd taken the only chance they'd had for escape and made a run for it. Banked on the fact that they hadn't tied her up and that it might mean they weren't willing to hurt her and Nate.

Did I make a horrible mistake?

"Mom."

She saw a white fence rail. "Climb over."

Her son hopped over it. He'd always been independent and never seemed to mind being alone. She hoped tonight didn't change that.

She launched herself at it but the sole of her boot slipped and she felt her shin slide over the wood. Jennie hissed out a breath. She forced the pain away and climbed regardless, the same way she took care of her son even when she had a migraine. Or got up and went to work in the barn, where she fired her pottery, when she was beyond exhausted. The way she saved one twenty-dollar bill every month for Christmas those times things were tight.

Because she was a mom, and that was what moms did.

He waited for her on the other side. She dropped down.

Behind her, she heard the man roar as he raced down the yard. Another man exited the house, his face shadowed against the yellow light from inside.

"Go." Jennie grabbed his hand.

Nate's was already there, fingers curling around hers. So much trust.

They disappeared together into the dark of night. Above them an ocean of stars she'd always loved. This land. The places her mother had walked, and the things she'd showed Jennie before she'd died.

The God she had introduced Jennie to.

Help us.

Those men would catch up. She and Nate needed a hiding place, but there was nothing out here. Mountains stretched up to the right, as though they could touch the night sky above through sheer force of will. To the left, her town sat at the bottom of the valley. Between, there was only desert.

No houses. Not even a tree.

Cold air seeped into her jeans and the thin sweater she wore over her T-shirt. Nate was in his pajamas, as he'd been just out of the bath when the men had burst in. She'd made them wait so he could get shoes and she could tug her boots on.

A gunshot rang out, over to her left.

Too far aside to have been someone intending to shoot them. Were they trying to force her to stop by frightening her? She couldn't let that happen.

"Come on." She was babbling and repeating herself.

"I'm going as fast as I can." His words were breathy.

"I know." Jennie tried to tamp down the fear.

Her shin cried out with every step, shooting fire up her leg, and she thought she might be bleeding. She wanted to tell him she was sorry. So sorry.

She'd worked so hard to keep Nate from the life she had lived as a child. Surrounded by the worst of humanity, people who bought illegal substances and sold those drugs to whomever would buy them.

Now the past had finally caught up to her.

Her leg nearly gave out. She had to stop soon, or she would simply collapse. They needed a place to hide.

Jennie pulled in a long breath and tried to think.

Another shot rang out, far to her right.

She flinched and let out a squeak. Her son whimpered, and she thought he might be crying. Her heart broke, hearing that sound.

Jennie stumbled. She caught herself before she landed on her injured shin and saw the shinnery oak beside her. *Nate.*

She grasped him in a hug and rolled, ducked behind the bush. *God, hide us.*

"Where'd they go?"

Nate sucked in a breath. She tugged him closer, wrapping her arms snugly around his little body. He tucked himself against her. Knees pulled up, hands grasping the sleeves of her sweater. She would thank God every day for the rest of their lives that she had him sleep in fleece-lined sweats and a long-sleeved shirt in winter even though he complained he got sweaty at night.

If they even survived this.

A male voice said, "I don't see them."

Jennie hugged her son and just breathed.

"Go back to the house. Get two flashlights and call it in."

"You wanna tell the boss we lost them? He'll kill us."

"Then don't call in. Fetch the lights and get back out here. I'll need help bringing them to the house after we knock 'em out and hog-tie 'em."

Nate sniffed, tight against her chest.

Jennie touched her lips to the side of his cheek. He was cold. Hungry.

"Fine."

She heard the one leave. That left the other—the one who wanted to tie them up—close by. Jennie figured they'd reached this far by just going for it. They could do that again.

Move and risk him hearing her, or stay and risk him finding them?

Nate squeezed her arm. She figured that meant she should loosen her grip on him. He shifted a fraction but didn't go anywhere. Best kidnapping buddy ever. She'd loved him fiercely since the day she'd learned she was pregnant. Now she thought she loved him even more.

A twig snapped.

They both gasped, tiny noises that sounded like a hundred twenty decibels in the night.

The man moved off, circling around.

When she thought he was far enough away, Jennie tapped her son's back. He shifted off her lap so she could get her feet under her and crouch. Ready to spring into action and defend him to the death.

And she would die.

This man had a gun. Whether he intended to kill her or recapture her didn't matter. She would come out of this only one way if she challenged him.

The moonlight illuminated enough that she could see. A night like this, she knew if they stayed out it would be as bright as daylight with only natural radiance once their eyes adjusted. The minute the other guy showed up with flashlights, all that would be gone.

The man was moving away.

They could head in the other direction, crest the side of this mountain and get to the road. Head back toward town. Flag down a motorist, praying it wouldn't be one of these guys.

Nate squeezed her hand.

She tugged on his.

They moved together, racing up the hill at an angle. Around a bush. She prayed they wouldn't twist an ankle in some creature's hole as they ran and ran, every step farther from that man and his gun.

On the far side of the mountain, the terrain fell away. Jennie gasped. They angled left, taking some animal's worn path.

And then Jennie's foot slipped. The sand slid out from under her, and she fell. Out of instinct, she let go of Nate's hand before she dragged him down, too.

Jennie tumbled end-over-end down the mountain to the tune of her son's heart-shattering cry.

"Mom!"

That had been a child's cry. State police officer Patrick Sanders glanced across the open desert at the base of a mountain.

Had he found what he was looking for?

Tucker sniffed, nose turned to the breeze.

Patrick's K-9 partner, an Airedale terrier he'd gotten from a shelter as a puppy and trained, scented the wind. His body stiffened and he leaned forward. As an air-scent dog, Tucker didn't need a trail to follow. He could catch the scent he was looking for on the wind, or in this case, the winter breeze rolling over the mountain, and search a general area.

Patrick's mountains, the place he'd grown up. Until right before his high school graduation when his mom had packed them up and fled town. They'd lost their home and everything they'd had there.

Including the girl Patrick had loved.

He didn't want to think about her, or what her father had said to him. Patrick shook his head. *Too bad.* He wouldn't get what he wanted. There was no way to not think about her, because Jennie Wilson was the woman he was out here looking for.

He heard another cry. Stifled by something; it was hard to hear as it drifted across so much open terrain.

He and his K-9 had been dispatched to find Jennie and her son Nathan. A friend had reported them missing yesterday, and the sheriff wasted no time at all calling for a search and rescue team from state police.

It figured a girl like her had grown up and gotten married—even if she'd kept her maiden name—and she'd had a child. She had been beautiful in high school, both a good and bad thing. He'd been too young to deal with feelings of that magnitude. Turned out, she was the only woman he'd ever loved.

Was it the son who had called out? It had sounded like a child.

The danger was now. He didn't need to get mired in a past that was nothing but a bittersweet memory to keep him warm on this chilly night. It was January and a cold wind blew through the desert, making thirty-eight degrees feel like twenty-eight. He shivered beneath the collar of his jacket while Tucker trotted ahead on a mission.

The dog had caught a scent and was closing in. The curly fluff on his body shifted as he moved.

Patrick let the Airedale's coat grow out a little in the winter. Not that Tucker worried much about extreme temperatures. He loved ninety degrees as much as he loved snow. Patrick had also never met a dog so happy to be given a task.

As a terrier, it was about the challenge. Tucker had proved to be both prey driven—like fetching a ball—or food driven—like a nice piece of chicken, or even a raw carrot sometimes—when he felt like it. Life was to be lived on his terms, which kept Patrick on his toes, needing to be as in sync with the dog as possible. Sometimes all Tucker wanted as a reward was a second of praise for a job well done and he was good.

Life with Tucker was like a constant conversation.

Right now the dog had to find Jennie and the boy so Patrick could transport them to safety. Then he intended to get out of town again. Back to his life in Albuquerque and studying for the sergeant's exam.

Tucker tugged harder on the leash, a signal the scent was stronger. He was closing in. Patrick's night of searching for the missing woman and her child would soon be over.

Tucker rounded a sagebrush and sat.

"Good boy. Yes, you are." Patrick let the leash slacken a little. He circled his dog and found her, lying on the ground.

"Jennie."

She stirred. Her eyes flashed open and she cried out.

"No, no." Right now he was just a dark figure leaning over her. "State police. I'm a K-9 officer." Most people softened when confronted with a police dog in a search and rescue situation. "I'm Officer Sanders."

He would get into the rest of it later. After she recognized him.

"Sanders?"

He helped her sit up. "Easy." He crouched, and Tucker leaned over to sniff without breaking his sit.

"This is Tucker. He's a search and rescue dog, here to find you and your son, Nathan."

She gasped. "Nate. I let go of him when I fell. Those men…" She scrambled to her feet, nearly knocking him over. "They're probably still up there. How far did I fall?"

She spun around.

Patrick said, "Sheriff Johns called us here to help find you both. It's our job." He motioned to his dog and figured he'd be reassuring. "Finding people is Tucker's favorite thing to do. He loves kids."

"Patrick."

"Yes, Jennie. It's me." Did she have a concussion? Maybe he should call for a helicopter to fly her to the hospital, but she wasn't swaying or slurring her words.

"You're really here."

He nodded.

"We need to find Nate."

"I have a T-shirt from your house. Tucker can get the scent and find your son."

She blinked. "He's—"

Patrick finished for her. "Nine years old and up there with armed men, right? In danger." He grasped her elbow. "So let's go."

The quicker he got them both to safety, the quicker he'd be able to leave town again.

For good this time.

She stood, seemingly steady enough on her feet. Determined to get to her child. He grabbed the evidence bag from the side pocket of his cargo pants and let his dog smell the contents.

"Tucker, find."

TWO

Tucker set off. The long leash snapped tight and Patrick followed at a brisk pace.

Jennie had to hustle to keep up. Her legs didn't want to move that fast, but she forced them to stick with the harsh pace. *Nate.* Jennie prayed with every step as they climbed up the side of the mountain.

She was so tired. Her head throbbed, and she could feel the sticky wet on her leg. But did that matter, when her son was out there somewhere? He was either alone on the mountain in the dark, or he'd been caught. Dragged back to that house. Or taken somewhere else at gunpoint.

And now this man in front of her showed up? Of all the people in the world, the love of her life—or so she'd thought at one point—was the responding police officer.

Nate.

Patrick might be here, but her son was all that mattered.

Your son.

Did he not know? How was it even possible that Patrick seemed to have no clue Nate was his son?

He'd talked to her father before he left.

The boy Rick Sanders, whom she'd known in high school, was no more. This was a man, Patrick Sanders the police officer. His youthful features had matured into handsome ones, catching her attention now far more than ever. Or she'd hit her head. Yet she couldn't help but notice he looked…strong.

Jennie had been relying on herself, and God's strength, since the day he'd left town. She didn't need a man in her life now. No, what she needed was Officer Sanders and his K-9 with the vest that read Search and Rescue.

Tucker sniffed the air as he battled his way up the steep trail. Every step the animal took was like a competitive athlete going after that gold medal while he dragged Patrick along. The dog's shaggy coat looked warmer than her thin sweater and he was focused in a way that made her think he was on an adventure. The animal seemed to love his job.

She'd been about to explain exactly who Nate was before Patrick had cut her off, reminding her that finding Nate was the priority here. Was he being purposely obtuse?

He was right, though. They had to find Nate. He was probably so scared.

That had nothing to do with the fact Patrick clearly hadn't wanted to be there for her when she'd found out she was pregnant. In fact, he'd left town without even talking to her. Telling her father that he wasn't interested in being part of her life anymore. Her dad, the criminal, had vowed to stick with her through it while the best guy she'd ever known had deserted her.

Talk about a slap in the face.

As soon as this job was done, he would no doubt leave all over again. He'd moved on to bigger and better things, this town nothing but a memory.

The thought of him having a new family slashed through her worse than any knife.

She looked for a ring on his left hand, but he wore gloves. Maybe he had a wife. A family. He wouldn't need Nate, or Jennie, in his life. Another woman wouldn't want an old girlfriend and her son showing up.

A whimper worked its way up her throat. Maybe it was better if she let him go on believing Nate wasn't his, and then he would just leave. Life would go back to normal. That might not be fair to him, but it would certainly be easier for her. Why did doing the right thing always have to be so hard?

"Come on, Jennie." He sounded irritated.

She started to reply, but her foot caught on something and she went down. Her injury smarted and she cried out in pain.

"Tuck!" Patrick barked the dog's name as a command.

She looked up. The dog stopped and turned, looking about as impatient as Patrick. She clambered to her feet, Patrick there holding her elbow.

"Quickly but carefully, okay?"

She nodded.

"We'll find your son."

The words cut through her. *Nate.* It didn't matter if Patrick had no interest in him. The two of them were a team, and they would get through this.

He looked down at her, then knelt. "You're bleeding."

She winced as he shifted her pant leg. "It's fine. We need to get Nate back."

He stood. "You're sure?"

She nodded, and man and dog set off again. In the moonlight, she saw the outline of his gun and shuddered, even though he was a cop.

She looked up at the hill beside them, the steep incline. She groaned. "How far did I roll?"

Surely, the house where they'd been held was just over

this ridge. She would get Nate back, give him the biggest hug ever and promise nothing bad would happen to him again. That wasn't realistic, but it didn't mean she wouldn't believe every word she said.

As the dog climbed the hill, practically dragging Patrick behind him, Jennie followed. She kept her gaze on the back of Patrick's jacket.

Walking away. Her going after him. The same way she'd done so many times in high school—the girl with the criminal father and a crush on the football captain, the golden boy. So her life had basically been a giant cliché, which occasionally she thought was amusing. When she wasn't angry at him for leaving her alone and pregnant.

He'd known what her father had been like, and yet Patrick hadn't even told her himself that he didn't care about the baby. He'd left it to her father to give her that message.

Clearly, Patrick's only concern here was getting this assignment done as fast as possible. Hot anger roiled in her empty stomach. But it was better than fear. Fear left a person powerless. Anger was like taking back control. Though, that wasn't more than an illusion, whereas fear was *very* real right now.

God, help me find Nate. Help him not be scared. Don't let him get hurt.

It wasn't Nate's fault that the land they lived on was useful to bad men. Drug traffickers. Neither was it his fault that Jennie had refused to allow them to cross her land. She didn't want armed bad guys anywhere near her son. Thinking they could do whatever they wanted when it was *her* property. She had a right to keep her son safe.

First, she'd called the sheriff. He'd driven out half a dozen times and had even spoken with men on her land. They'd told him they were merely lost. The last time, she'd called the Drug Enforcement Agency.

She was still waiting for a callback.

And then this happened?

Being taken from their house and held at gunpoint was a clear message. *Let us do what we want. Or else.*

She needed to get Nate back before she lost everything good in her life.

Tucker had the scent. He could smell the boy on the wind, and knew he was close by. Now it was just a case of the dog tracking it to the source, where the scent would be strongest. How he could tell the difference between her son Nate's smell in the air, or what was likely embedded in Jennie's clothing, Patrick didn't know. A canine's capacity to differentiate scents was fascinating.

And not something he needed to be distracted by right now. Though that would be better than the full force of being here with Jennie.

Never mind that he'd dreamed of her a million times over the years. He'd even thought about contacting her a few—thousand—times.

He didn't need to lose focus when Tucker was on the long line, working. Still, it was part of Patrick's makeup as a cop to ensure the victim present with him was all right.

"How are you doing back there?" He glanced over his shoulder.

She had on jeans, cowgirl boots and a thin sweater that probably wasn't doing much to ward off the cold.

"I'm…" She hugged herself. "I'll be good when we get to Nate." She glanced up the hill again.

She was bleeding. Might have even hit her head. She'd said something about falling, but she still wasn't slurring her words, so she likely didn't have a concussion.

He'd hear all about what happened in the hospital,

when she got medical attention. Safe. Sound. Her and her son.

Why did helping them seem different than what he did for any other person he'd ever helped as a cop?

Patrick didn't have the time to think about it too much. He pulled off his jacket and tucked it around her shoulders, which allowed her to pick up her pace to match the dog's.

By his side now, she said, "I thought dogs weren't supposed to pull on the leash."

"When he's working, it's all about tension. If I let it slacken, he'll lose focus."

"And this is what you do? Rescue people."

Patrick said, "Sometimes. We also go into situations where there may be bad guys hiding, and Tucker will find and flush them out. Recently we did a training course set up like a disaster zone. Tucker is certified to go in when there's been an earthquake or a building collapse. He can be sure-footed even when the terrain is unstable and still find his man."

"Must be nice," she muttered.

"We will find Nate." He glanced up at the top of the hill. Close now. Both of them were breathless. He was sweating, despite giving away his jacket. Most people preferred to be distracted. "We were specifically requested by Sheriff Johns because he knows what Tucker and I can do. And because I know the terrain."

She said nothing.

He acknowledged to himself that the terrain here was definitely proving unstable. And he wasn't talking about the mountain.

Too many of his memories were associated with the town at the bottom of the ridge. Mistakes. Things both of them would probably rather forget. After all, they'd built lives. Separate ones, after vowing they would never part.

He blew out a breath.

Tucker's head snapped to the side.

Patrick watched as the dog picked up on something then let out a low growl.

"What is it?" Jennie whispered.

"I don't know." But he had a free hand poised to reach for his gun nonetheless.

"God, keep him safe."

She whispered the words, and he knew they weren't for him. It seemed too intimate for him to be part of her private prayers. Did she believe now? Good for her that she had faith to fall back on at a time like this.

He'd left his faith behind a long time ago. Right around the time he'd been torn from her life, unable to come back. Not that she'd wanted him anymore. All they'd had? She'd tossed it aside the second things got hard. No longer interested. So he'd walked away from everything.

It had been the most painful experience of his life.

"He's all alone." Her soft voice carried to him on the breeze. But reassuring her could only go so far. He had to find her son. It was the only thing that would truly give her peace right now.

Tucker crested the ridge.

Patrick clicked his tongue and got the dog's attention. They crouched at the edge, side by side, and looked over.

"That's the house." She pointed to a structure tucked against the hillside to his left. A floodlight had been turned on, illuminating the yard, which was nothing more than the same sandy dirt and scrub brushes.

Except for a truck parked out front. Engine running. Door open so the dome light was on but there was no one inside.

"How many men were there?"

She sucked in a breath. "Two that I saw. But I thought I heard more voices than that." Fear lived in the quaver of her voice.

He'd never known what it felt like to be so scared and hoped for her sake that her son would come out of this unscathed. If Patrick could help him through it—before he left town when they were safe again and he was back in Albuquerque—then he'd do what he could. Maybe it would be enough to keep the kid from having nightmares.

"How many rooms?"

She briefly described the layout, but it sounded like she'd seen only part of the house. "I'm sorry. They shoved us in one room, and then when we left we just found the closest door and ran for it."

"Why did they want you? Did they say—"

The back door swung open.

One man strode out, dragging a smaller person with him. A child.

Her hand grasped his arm. To get his attention or for solidarity? He didn't know. She whispered, "Rick."

The name she used to call him, so long ago. There wasn't time to absorb the way it reassured him. Warmed him, even.

"We have to get him."

"I will." He watched the man tug the boy along toward the truck. "Stay here." Patrick unclipped Tucker's leash and dropped it to the ground. Then he clicked his tongue again and patted his leg.

Tucker moved with him, keeping beside Patrick's leg in a perfect heel, where he tracked with every footstep Patrick made.

There was no time to call for backup or check if he even had a cell signal right now. If he and Tucker were going to take this guy down and get the boy out of harm's way it would be together. In lockstep.

They were partners. Each watching the other's back.

Patrick kept his head low, weapon drawn, in a jog that ate up the sandy dirt between him and the truck. Jennie's son.

He'd have only a split second to react when the man saw him. Patrick would have to take that second and use it to his advantage. Act before the man could hurt Nate.

The gunman shoved Nate toward the truck.

The boy cried out, a sound that rang across the mountainside as clear as the night sky.

Patrick took two more steps and brought his gun up just as another man emerged from the house.

"Hey!" Jennie screamed down at the house. "Hey, I'm right here! Come and get me!"

Patrick nearly faltered. What was she doing?

"Mom!" The boy screamed for her, the sound so full of fear that it hurt to hear.

A gunshot rang out, whizzing above Patrick's head.

He hit the dirt and Jennie screamed.

THREE

She hit the ground and dirt wafted into her mouth. Jennie spat, getting back up to her knees immediately. "Nate!"

Patrick was already up, staying low as he ran toward her son with the dog close to his side. Headed right for the man with the gun. "State police! Put it down. On the ground. Put the gun down, now!"

She didn't even have a gun and she wanted to obey him. His voice carried that much command.

The gunman with her son froze. Nate cowered by the truck wheel, the engine still running. It hurt to see him so scared, even as her brain reminded her that it was good he'd curled into a smaller target. Patrick might not know who the boy was to him. *Should have told him.* But he would protect Nate.

"I said, put it down!"

She caught movement to her left, out the corner of her eye. Another gunman had emerged from the house. She couldn't make out his features, but the stance wasn't friendly. The second man held a gun in one hand, down by his side. Had Patrick seen…

"Hands on your head!" Busy ensuring their safety by disarming the first bad guy, Patrick hadn't even acknowledged Nate yet.

The man by the house raised his weapon.

Jennie grasped a palm-size rock and stood, hefting it as she rose so that the rock sailed across the distance between them and hit the second man square in the chest. *Thank you, softball.* The man yelped and staggered back.

His gun went off as he reeled. Patrick fired a round of his own, causing the man to pitch forward and stumble down the stairs. The gunman toppled to the ground, where he lay moaning. Patrick glanced from the bad guy beside him to the one at the house.

But it was too late.

The man by him launched up and into the front seat of the truck. He hit the gas and the vehicle lurched forward.

Nate dove out of the way, and Jennie had to watch in horror as the truck raced past. The wheel, so close. She tore down the mountainside to her son. He hit the ground, well clear of the truck as it sped closer to the house.

"Thank You, God. Thank You." She fell to her knees and gathered up her son in her arms as she watched the second man, the one Patrick had shot. The last thing she wanted was for any of them to get a bullet in their back.

Nate was safe—or would be in a second. That was what counted right now. The rest would come later, when she figured out why Patrick didn't seem to think Nate had anything to do with him. She wondered why he didn't know Nate was clearly his son. He'd known she was pregnant the night he left town, right?

The truck slowed. Patrick raced toward it, Tucker running fast beside him. Jennie watched as the second man, the one she'd hit with the rock, clambered up and hauled himself over the side of the truck, narrowly landing in the bed.

Patrick yelled after them but didn't shoot.

Jennie almost wanted him to. These men had kidnapped her. They'd terrorized Nate.

She twisted to look down at him, then shuffled the boy in her arms to lay him down. "Patrick!"

He ran over, commanding the dog to "guard" as he dropped to his knees beside her. "What is it?" Patrick grabbed something from his belt. He flipped a switch and the flashlight illuminated. He moved it so the side of the beam lit up her son's face. "He's unconscious?"

Jennie just nodded as tears rolled down her face. "He must have rolled and hit his head on something. I thought he was just getting out of the way of the truck."

He squeezed her shoulder. "I'll call for—I have no signal."

"It's spotty up here." She patted Nate's face. "Baby, wake up. Mama's here." He didn't like her calling him "baby" since he considered himself a big kid these days. A young man, even. He puffed up when the pastor called him that.

"Maybe there's a phone in the house?"

She didn't know if Patrick wanted an answer to his question. She kept patting Nate's cheek, praying at the same time that he'd just passed out for a second. Shock, not a concussion. "Come on, Nate. Wake up."

He moaned and shifted, his eyes fluttering.

"Hey." When she saw his eyes fully open, Jennie couldn't help but smile. "There you are." She touched her forehead to his, then kissed him, being careful to keep it light just in case he'd hit the back of his head. "Hi, baby."

His brows drew together. She saw the objection in his eyes before he'd even finished the thought and knew then he didn't have a concussion.

"I know. Don't call you 'baby.' Give your mother a break, okay? It's been a long day." She sat back out of sheer relief, toppled over and wound up slumped against Patrick. Snug in his coat. No gunmen in sight. She was almost giddy, even though they were miles from anywhere with no way to get there except their legs.

Thank You, God.

Nate sat up.

Both of them reached for him. Patrick said, "Easy."

Nate stiffened. "Are you…?"

"I'm a cop." Patrick shone the flashlight on the badge clipped to his belt. "And this is Tucker. He's a cop, too. He's the one who found you after your mom—"

"You fell down the mountain!"

"I know." Jennie groaned, and all the fear and grief rushed back. She didn't know what to do with it and more tears rolled down her face. She gathered her son to her in a hug and reveled in the feel of him.

"I thought you…" His voice thickened and he coughed.

"What happened after?" She leaned back to look at him. She had to know. "Did they hurt you?"

"One of them grabbed my arm and dragged me back to the house." Tears trailed down his face, too, and Patrick handed her a pack of tissues from one of the pockets of his cargo pants.

"He said the boss didn't care about you. He wanted to see *me*. Why, Mom? I don't want to see him."

Jennie touched the sides of his face. "No one is going to take you from me. He didn't, right? I was here. So was Patrick, and Tucker."

Nate's gaze flicked to the man beside her and she saw him make the connection. Yep. He'd heard the name Patrick before. That was her smart little boy.

She said, "You're safe now, right?"

He nodded.

"Tell me what happened."

"You saved me. You, and Patrick. And Tucker." Nate motioned to the dog, who lifted his head. Ears pricked.

Patrick said, "That's right."

Nate stared at him.

Tucker inched forward, his belly still on the ground. He sniffed and then licked Nate's arm. Her son jerked and then chuckled. Sounding more like the little boy from a few years ago than the third-grader she had on her hands nowadays.

Patrick said a soft, high-pitched "Yes" directed at Tucker.

The dog lifted to stand, his face level with Nate's. In one long swipe, he licked Nate from his chin to his hairline.

The boy erupted into laughter, winding his arms around the dog's neck. She saw Patrick give Tucker a hand signal and figured with the open palm that he'd asked the dog to stand still for a hug.

Her heart melted.

No matter what they'd been through tonight, she was glad for this moment. God had brought Patrick and his dog here. Something that had made Nate laugh. They offered more comfort than she could provide right now. *Thank You, Lord.* It was an unexpected gift she would be forever grateful for. Regardless of how things might turn out, this meeting had been sweet.

"Patrick…" she began, no clue how she was going to ask him why he didn't seem to care, or maybe even re-alize, that Nate was his son. Maybe this wasn't the time for that conversation anyway.

Before she could continue, he stood. "I'm going to check the house for a phone. Tucker, guard."

Patrick made a quick search of the house. Thankfully it was small, barely larger than a cabin. Jennie and Nate had spent hours here, fearing for their lives, while two men with guns burned coffee in the kitchen.

He wanted to see me.

The boy's words reverberated in his mind. The gunmen had been waiting for something. Or, more likely, *someone.* If they'd had no cell signal, the two men had likely hung here waiting for their boss or some other person to arrive. After that, who knew what would have happened?

He didn't want to know and was glad it hadn't come to that.

Patrick wrinkled his nose at the coffeepot on the counter—the source of that smell—and headed back out, more than ready to personally guard Jennie and her son.

He strode back to them. "No phone inside. We'll have to walk to my car. I'll drive you two back to town, to the hospital."

Jennie nodded.

Patrick crouched in front of the boy. "You okay, buddy?"

The edge of fear was still in Nate's eyes. "Are you really a cop?"

Patrick could understand Nate's hesitation to go with him—a stranger with a gun—after being held by two of them. Yes, he was far different than those men. He had a badge, after all. But fear wasn't normally rational.

He kept his voice soft. "I am a cop. I know you're scared, but Tucker and I are going to make sure you and your mom get to safety. No more bad guys, okay?"

Nate nodded, relief in his eyes. "Okay."

Patrick glanced at Jennie. She looked like she wanted to say something, and he figured he knew what it was. Something that might put the boy's mind at ease.

"You know what?" Patrick asked. "Your mom and

I are actually old friends. We knew each other in high
school."

"Your name's Patrick?"

Jennie said, "Um…maybe we should…" Could be she
was embarrassed because she'd done nothing, said nothing, when her father had run Patrick and his mom out
of town.

Patrick glanced at her son. "Yes. I'm Patrick."

The boy stared up at him. "Patrick is my dad's name."
He then looked to his mom.

Patrick just stared at the little boy.

He heard Jennie whisper, "Rick."

The name, *her* name for him, sliced like a blade. He
sucked in a breath and turned to her. "What…?" He
couldn't formulate a question. Didn't even know what
to say.

"Patrick…"

He glanced at her. "What…is this?"

"This—" she touched the boy's shoulder while the kid
looked up at him with wide eyes "—is your son. Our son.
The one my father told you about before you left town."

Patrick stared at Jennie. Her father had told him…
what?

Jennie blinked. "Please say something."

He had a son?

Or was he supposed to ask "Why didn't you tell me?"
or "Why didn't you try to find me?" Patrick couldn't
voice either, and didn't know if he should in front of a
son he hadn't even known about.

"He ran me and my mother out of town."

"Which left me alone and pregnant." The hurt on her
face was apparent.

When he hadn't even known anything about this?

His brain couldn't catch up to what was happening, let alone have a coherent thought right now.

All this time. I had a son.

Did she think he wouldn't have stuck around? Or asked her to *go with him*? He'd done one of those, suggesting she run with him, but she'd chosen her father out of fear.

And she'd raised her son in the town where that man—her own father—sold drugs.

"I'm guessing your father just *loves* the fact I'm his grandson's dad."

Nate's face dissolved.

Jennie sucked in a breath.

Patrick wanted to call the words back. As if that was even possible. "I'm sorry. I'm sure you all have a wonderful time at family dinners."

Now he was making it worse.

Tucker whined.

Patrick rolled to his heels and stood. "It's best if we head to my car. We can talk on the way, okay?" He held out his hand to Nate. What did he say to a boy he'd just met, who was his son? He was in shock.

Thankfully the boy took his hand and Patrick helped him to his feet. He didn't let go of the kid's hand. Instead, he shook it. As though this were some kind of official meeting, and they weren't standing outside an abandoned house after he'd been kidnapped.

"It's really nice to meet you, Nate." Patrick meant it. Regardless of what Jennie had done, the years she'd denied him the chance to know his own child—and how that made him feel—the boy didn't deserve to be in the middle of that. She'd known she was pregnant and she'd still chosen to stay with her father?

This was unbelievable. He deserved an explanation, but that would have to come later. When they were safe.

Patrick crouched so he was nearly eye level with the boy. "I'm glad you're all right, and that I could be the one to make sure you're safe."

"It's…nice to meet you, too."

Patrick straightened and Nate stared up at him.

"Am I gonna be as tall as you?"

Jennie touched his shoulder. "If you are, you'll eat me out of house and home. I'll be broke." She laughed, but Patrick didn't totally believe she thought this was funny. Still, he knew her attempt at humor worked when Nate relaxed and turned to her.

"I'm having a growth spurt."

"You're *always* having a growth spurt."

Patrick grinned, not really feeling it but needing to do what was best to put Nate at ease right now. When he glanced at Jennie, he saw the same need in her eyes. The times she'd smiled for her son, or reassured him, when circumstances were far from good.

"Are you okay to walk?"

Nate nodded. Jennie said, "I think so." She touched her temple. "My head hurts, but I'd rather get out of here."

Patrick snapped the leash back on Tucker and then led the way, the two of them behind him. Holding hands. Reminding him they had a connection without him. He'd been denied knowing his son, while they'd lived for years sharing that bond of family and unconditional love.

Jennie had lied to him, withholding the fact she was pregnant the last time they'd spoken. Then she hadn't even responded to his letters.

She'd basically told him she'd wanted nothing to do with him. Then he'd made his last-ditch effort to convince her, and she'd had her father try to pay him off while he ran Patrick's mother out of town in a grab for her land.

Now it made sense. Jennie had known she was pregnant. Her father had offered him a payout. Money Patrick hadn't accepted and was certain her father would never have parted with anyway. Because her father had wanted him out of the picture? He'd wanted to… What? Raise the boy himself?

Patrick shuddered. He'd been manipulated.

There was far too much bad blood between him and Jennie to ever salvage anything from their past, despite the fact the attraction remained.

She and Nate could have died tonight. He was tempted to thank God he'd been the one sent here. But he didn't believe anymore.

A loving God would never have allowed Patrick to leave town not knowing Jennie was pregnant with his baby. Her father had wanted Patrick out of her life but had never gone that far before. Patrick now understood why he'd suddenly been willing to part with so much money just to get rid of him. Patrick hadn't accepted the money. Her father had been so eager to see him gone.

Patrick was going to make sure he had the relationship with his son that he'd always wanted with his father. Someone who made him feel safe and loved.

That was what he'd tried to give Jennie, in his own way. How many times had he told her they'd needed to get away from her father?

Now, he didn't want anything to do with her. He would be Nate's father, but Jennie was not going to be part of Patrick's life.

Not after what she'd done, keeping the truth from him.

"Patrick!"

The second she called out, he realized why. A vehicle made its way up the road, headed for the house.

"Come on. Nate, Jennie. We need to run!"

FOUR

He didn't even care. Jennie could think of nothing else. She was right. He'd acted shocked, but that was probably only for Nate's benefit. She kept hold of her son's hand as they hustled to Patrick's car.

Every sound. Every shuffle, or snap. Jennie whirled around, expecting a gunman. Meanwhile, beside her, Nate walked straight. Eyes straight. Body taut.

They'd finally outrun their pursuers.

She squeezed Nate's hand. "Hey. You okay?"

He nodded, and a million questions roiled through her head. Why had they been taken? Who was behind it? What had they been waiting for? Who was the "boss" and what did he want with Nate?

"Hungry?"

No answer.

"Yeah, me neither," Jennie said. "Hot chocolate, though. Now that sounds like a good idea."

He exhaled, and she might've seen a flash of a smile. Her eyes had readjusted to the darkness so she could make out her son's features.

Him. Her. They were the whole world as far as she was concerned. They had Jesus, so what else did they need?

Some might think that was a cliché, but for the two of them it was everything.

The man walking with his dog in front of them, leading them away from danger, wasn't part of their lives.

She figured Patrick probably had as many questions in his mind as she did. Yes, they'd sprung the news on him at a bad moment. Not the worst, just bad. Compassion meant she should try to see things from his side, but the truth was that he hadn't wanted to know. Why be so surprised about his son now? It didn't make any sense to her. Obviously a nine-year-old boy was his. What kind of a girl did he think she had been back then?

Her father's daughter.

She hadn't been that girl since her dad had died. Since her brother had joined the army and never written. Never called. Jennie had long since realized she had no one but herself and Nate.

The last time she'd tried to find Patrick, she'd gone so far as to hire a private investigator. Never mind that Patrick hadn't seemed to want to know. It was the right thing to offer him a relationship with his son.

The investigator had happily taken a chunk of her inheritance money. A few weeks later he emailed to say he hadn't been able to find Patrick Moreno.

Officer Sanders.

No wonder, considering he'd changed his name. Why had he done that? Though, shouldn't a private investigator worth his salt be able to find someone even after a name change? If he'd been in witness protection, or something, Patrick would never have come back. But he had. So how hard could it have been to find him?

Apparently, she'd just needed to be kidnapped.

"Mom."

She glanced down, realizing she was squeezing her son's hand too hard. "Sorry, bud."

Patrick clicked the locks on his small SUV. He loaded Tucker in the back, and then held the door while Nate and Jennie both climbed into the back seat.

When he got in, he turned and asked, "Are you cold, Nate?"

"A little."

Patrick stared at him for another second, as though absorbing the sight of a boy he now knew was his son.

I'm sorry. The words stuck in her throat.

No matter what justification she felt for the fact he hadn't known about Nate, she did feel guilty he didn't seem to have known. He'd been genuinely surprised, flipping upside down everything she thought she understood about what had happened the night he'd left.

What her father had told her.

He really hadn't known she was pregnant?

Patrick started his vehicle and set the heater to full blast.

Jennie wound up taking off Patrick's jacket before they got to the hospital, where he turned to her. "You guys go in. I need to call the sheriff."

Jennie shoved the door open. As Nate climbed out, the dog whined, his nose against the wire that divided the seats from the trunk area.

Nate said, "Bye, Tucker."

Patrick glanced over. She knew that look on his face. The first expression that even resembled the boy he'd been. Sure, his features were the same. But he'd grown up so much. Nine, nearly ten, years and he was…a man. A handsome man.

Nate and Jennie walked into the hospital and got checked in. When she mentioned they'd been kidnapped, the woman at the desk blinked then snapped up the phone. "I should call Sheriff Johns."

"He's already been called," Jennie said. "There's a cop outside. I think he'll be in shortly." She realized that she didn't know if Patrick was planning on coming in. He hadn't said that, specifically.

"He's my dad." Nate's chin lifted. "He's a *cop*, and he has a *police dog*."

The double doors whooshed open. Jennie turned and watched as Patrick strode in. Nate tugged at her hand. She let go, and he moved to his dad.

Jennie winced. But it was too late.

Nate slammed into Patrick, arms wrapping around his middle. Patrick lifted the boy up. Nate immediately tucked his head into his father's neck, one hand grasping Patrick's shirt.

"Ma'am."

Jennie spun around and saw the nurse.

"If you'll come this way."

She wasn't going anywhere without Nate. Jennie held out her hand…but Patrick would have to put him down. She dropped her hand to her side. Wow. She might actually be jealous. No, she was just exhausted. They'd been through a horrifying day.

"Let's get you seen to." The woman led her to a bed, surrounded by a curtain. "I'm sure your husband will take good care of your son."

Still, as the woman ushered her in, Jennie turned to Patrick and mouthed, *Be nice.*

He frowned and carried their son to the next bay. Jennie tugged on the curtain so she could see. Patrick laid Nate on the bed. He grasped for his father's hand and scooted over so Patrick could sit beside him on the bed.

It was the trauma. That was why he was latching on

to Patrick—who hadn't even looked at her. She'd told her son plenty of stories about his dad. After all, what child wouldn't be curious about an absent parent? He'd seen pictures of his father. Heard all the stories about Patrick's football team wins. Now Nate never missed a home game.

His father was here. Everything he'd ever wanted. And on a night like tonight? She didn't blame him for holding on tight. This man had rescued him.

So why did Jennie feel like she was going to be sick?

The doctor pulled back the curtain. "Nathan Patrick Wilson?"

Patrick stiffened, hearing his own name as his son's middle name. Nate stiffened as well, which he figured was for a whole different reason. Patrick shifted on the bed to face him. "Hey. The doctor just needs to make sure you're all right. Okay?"

Nate looked at him. "Mom's the one who's bleeding."

Maybe it was fear, or maybe he was the kind of male who needed the woman he cared about to be seen to first. Either way, the outcome was the same.

The doctor glanced at Jennie in the next bed over. Then he looked back at Nate. "That your mom, Nathan?"

The boy nodded.

"I'm going to have a nurse take a look at you while I look at your mom's leg. Is that good with you?"

"Yes."

Patrick figured the doctor had read Nate's wariness. That was a good quality in someone who needed to treat injuries and illnesses but also had to have a care for the emotions and mental state of his patient.

The nurse checked out Nate, who had a few scrapes and bruises along with a sprained wrist. It was the bump on the side of his head—one that neither Patrick nor Jennie had noticed in the dark—that worried both her and the doctor. Nate was admitted overnight, while Jennie was cleaned up. Her leg was bandaged, but her injured head needed pain pills.

She came over and sat on the end of Nate's bed.

The nurse gave the boy a shot to calm him so he could sleep and, minutes later, his eyes fluttered closed. He fought it. Struggling to stay awake. "Mom."

She leaned over and kissed his cheek. "Good night, buddy."

Patrick knew Nate had been in good hands with his mom. And yet she'd denied him the chance to know his son. "You should have told me."

"I thought you knew." She gritted her teeth, whispering back, "And I *still* tried to find you anyway. Now, right when we're kidnapped, here you are. Waltzing in with your *dog* to save the day. Well you can go back the way you came. We didn't need you before, and we don't need you now."

He laughed, but there was no humor in it. "Not happening."

She really thought he would leave when he'd just met Nate? No way. Seriously. *No. Way.* Not in a million years.

"So tell me why you were kidnapped, and maybe I can figure out exactly how much danger you put *my* son in."

She shook her head and got up. The second she put weight on her leg, she winced.

"Sit back down."

"Don't tell me what to do." She glared at him. "You chose to leave. I did the best I could, alone and pregnant, with no one but my *father* to ask for help." She kept her voice low, so she didn't wake Nate, but her tone dripped with angry sarcasm. "You can probably imagine how that went. But you don't know. Because you weren't there."

"Is he why you were kidnapped? Some kind of turf war?"

Her father was a drug dealer the sheriff hadn't managed to put in prison while Patrick was in high school. If things were the same, Jennie was probably still caught in the middle all the time. And Nate? Patrick didn't even want to imagine what back-and-forth the boy had been subjected to.

"That would be difficult. Since my father died when Nate was two. He doesn't even remember his grandfather, so I'd appreciate it if you quit bringing him up."

Her dad was dead?

"And you still didn't find me."

"That would be difficult, *Officer Sanders*. Considering I didn't even know your name. Why did you change it?"

Patrick said, "That's why I wrote you all those letters. So you'd know how to find me. In case you changed your mind, which is what I was hoping. But I never heard back from you."

"Maybe that's because I didn't get any letters."

He was about to reply in kind, his tone now hard as hers and just as sardonic. But Nate rolled over in his sleep and tucked himself against Patrick's side, his hand on Patrick's arm.

He stared down at those small fingers. Tiny nails, smaller than he'd ever seen. A scar on the knuckle, long since healed. Evidence that he'd lived a life.

One Patrick had missed.

Jennie said, "I tried to find you." After a pause, she added, "You knew where I was."

He'd also known who she'd lived with—a father who had no moral compass and an even lesser desire to do anything but make money by any means necessary.

He lifted his gaze to hers and saw tears in her eyes. "I didn't know I had a son."

Pain flashed in her eyes. He realized the implication of his words. He'd have come back for Nate, but not for her. The truth was, that had proved correct. He'd stayed away. Because of her father.

His mom had taken him to Albuquerque to stay with his aunt. Changed their names to his mom's maiden name, Sanders. She'd gotten a job as a waitress and he'd worked while going to school. Twice as hard as everyone else. Twice as determined to become a cop and put men like Jennie's father away.

"Now I do. Your secret is out, and I know about Nate."

Patrick had to let go of the pain. Get along with her, enough that Nate could have some semblance of a peaceful life as he was shuffled between his parents.

The curtain fluttered and a nurse appeared. She stepped aside to admit the sheriff.

Bitterness left a sour taste in Patrick's mouth, but he swallowed against it. "Sheriff Johns."

The old man nodded. "Officer Sanders. You found them. Good job." He glanced at Jennie.

She tried to smile.

Johns looked back at Patrick. "Everything okay?" He frowned. "Is Nathan okay?"

You mean, Nathan Patrick Wilson? He wondered if the old man knew he was Nate's father. Could be he'd planned this. Brought Patrick here, so he could meet them. Probably not. Maybe the reason was far more sinister.

Patrick turned to Jennie. "Tell me who those men that kidnapped you were."

Her mouth dropped open and she paled. "You think they'll come back?"

"Now, Officer—"

Patrick interjected, "I'm taking a witness statement, if you don't mind."

"I do mind." Johns rocked to the balls of his feet and then back. "You were brought here for one search and rescue job. You found them, and now they're good. You can go, Officer Sanders. Before I call your lieutenant in Albuquerque and tell him you overstayed your welcome in my town."

Patrick just stared at him.

What was going on?

FIVE

I *didn't know I had a son.*

Jennie wanted to collapse into the nearest chair and just cry. At least now he knew her father was gone.

She looked at her son, holding his hand while the sheriff and Officer Sanders—it was much better to think of him like that—duked it out over who was going to talk to her.

"Go ahead and call my lieutenant, Sheriff. I'll wait."

Jennie heard Patrick shift and glanced over to see he'd folded his arms. Determined. Refusing to back down. Exactly the kind of man Nate needed in his life. Someone who could teach him to be a good man. Patrick hadn't been there for her when she could have used that kind of man in her life. None of the other men around her had been anywhere near good. Not her dad. Not her brother.

Patrick had been the breath of fresh air she thought she'd needed back then, even if it hadn't lasted. In comparison, her brother, the train wreck, had disappeared just after he'd graduated high school—right before her junior year—and joined the army. She'd only seen Martin once since, but on several occasions he'd called, asking for money. One time he'd been in a jail cell in Georgia, needing to be bailed out. But all that was years ago. Until last summer, when the army called her a few times.

She hadn't called them back.

Martin hadn't been a part of her life for years, and she had no intention of inviting him in again now.

The sheriff's words cut through her thoughts. "—do you hope to achieve here? You've done your job."

"So you insist on pointing out."

Was he going to tell the sheriff that Nate was his son? Jennie didn't think that was any of the old man's business. Especially considering the way he'd tiptoed around the problems she'd been having out on her property.

Jennie twisted to face the sheriff. "I've asked Officer Sanders to help me and Nate." Yes, it would be because Nate was his son. And no, she hadn't specifically asked him. But Patrick was on board, even if he intended to blame her through the whole thing.

She continued. "The same men who've been trespassing on my land took me and my son from our house. They kept us overnight, trying to scare us. They chased us. They shot at us. And I think they were going to take us to meet someone." She folded her arms, trying not to talk so loudly she woke Nate. "I don't want them coming back, or trying again. I want Nate to be safe."

"It's over now," Johns said. "There's no reason to believe you're still in danger."

"And when they drive onto my back forty again, causing trouble, making noise and a mess? What then?" She didn't go there much. But that didn't mean she wanted bad guys on her land, or anywhere near her son. "I'm supposed to just let them do whatever they want?"

"They're still out there?" The sheriff glanced between her and Patrick.

"They ran off."

The sheriff huffed. As though Patrick should have saved the two of them *and* arrested those guys, as well. In the middle of a gunfight. "I thought you had a K-9 with you."

Patrick's lips pressed into a thin line.

Jennie wasn't interested in a battle between the local sheriff and Patrick, who represented the New Mexico State Police. What she wanted to know was why the sheriff had been blowing off her concerns for weeks now.

"Have you received any calls from the DEA?" Jennie asked. "I left all the information when I called them, but they never called me back."

The sheriff blinked. "You called the Drug Enforcement Agency?"

"Sheriff—"

Whatever Patrick had been about to say, the sheriff cut him off. "It's trespassers. That's a local problem, and it's going to have a local solution." He shook his head, looking exasperated. "Everyone knows those boys have dirty federal agents on their payroll. You probably tipped off these guys, and that's why they kidnapped you."

"I thought it was trespassers." Jennie tried to look innocent, with a side of oblivious. She wasn't sure it worked. "You're saying they could be drug runners? I know my father used to transport narcotics through town using back roads and people's land. I thought you shut all that down."

Also, since her father had died, a lot of his associates had scattered, leaving a void in town. The rest of what had happened to the drug trade locally…she had no idea. She'd been a busy twenty-year-old single mom trying to figure out how to make enough money to support herself and her son.

Sheriff Johns shrugged. "Who knows what kind of

men they were? Could just have been a couple of bikers, or transients. People looking for passage through
the back country."

"We know what kind of men they were." Patrick stared
down the sheriff. "Both Jennie and I saw their faces. So
we'll need you to supply us with your collection of mug
shots, and we're happy to ID them."

Jennie nodded. "Yes, we're happy to tell you who it
was. Then you can bring them in."

"Good." The sheriff didn't look like he thought that
would be a problem, but he also didn't seem happy, either.

She wasn't sure if he was on the up-and-up or not.
She'd always thought he was a good guy, or at least tried
to be. "Then there will be two fewer dangerous men out
there."

Johns nodded. "We try. Right, Officer Sanders? Every
day, chipping away at the bad element. The job is never
done but we do what we can to stem the tide. Especially
in a place like this, where good people live."

Maybe Johns thought *she* had something to do with it.
Like this was a turf war and she was some kind of drug
queen. Jennie would have been scared if that idea hadn't
made her want to laugh out loud.

"And," Patrick said, "we'll know who their associates
are as soon as we know their names. Which gives me a
shot to identify this boss they were going to take Jennie
and Nate to see."

Neither of them mentioned Nate being taken alone.
That would come, and she got the feeling Patrick was as
reticent to overshare with the sheriff as she was.

Sheriff Johns hadn't protected her. He'd only brushed
her off, insisting things weren't that bad. *Just a few high
school kids, Jennie. I'm sure of it.* Then they'd come to
her house at night.

She noticed Patrick's gaze on her. A slight frown shifted his brows, but she knew if she leaned into his concern, that would just give her permission to fall apart. And that was the last thing she needed to do right now... when she should be strong for Nate.

For Nate.

Patrick would make sure his son was safe, and that was all that mattered.

She was scared. Really scared. Patrick could see the fear on her face, and it made him want to protect her.

He pulled out his phone and typed a quick email to his partner, copying in their lieutenant. He needed Eric here to help him figure this out and he wanted the lieutenant to sign off on it. But he included the personal revelation. No point hiding the fact when he'd later ask for a vacation so he could get to know his son. He had enough accrued days that he would be able to take a couple of weeks off at least.

Judging by the look on Jennie's face, she wasn't going to say no to him hanging around. And if that meant he had his gun on his hip and his dog by his side, she'd probably feel a little better still.

He turned to the sheriff. "So you'll get me those mug shots?"

"Why wouldn't I?"

Patrick clenched his jaw. No point arguing with the man, even if he insisted on making everything a battle of wills. Was he just an old sheriff, set in his ways, or was there a reason Johns wanted to take care of this himself? Sounded like there wasn't. Or, if there was, the man was inordinately slow at getting results.

What was up with that?

Patrick needed more information if he was going to

figure out why those men had taken her and Nate, who their boss was and what it had to do with trespassers. But he would find out. Otherwise he'd have to go back to his office, and his home, knowing there was still danger on Jennie's land. Right at his son's doorstep.

"Great. I appreciate the aid," Patrick said. "I'll be sticking around to make sure both Nate and Jennie remain safe until the men that took them are behind bars. Along with everyone they work with."

No, he wasn't a one-man army. Still, he had every reason to see it through. Jennie wasn't married. She was doing this alone when she could have the bonus of someone else there to share the load. As it had been with his mom—also a single mom after his father had died—she very much *could* do it all by herself.

But that didn't mean she *had* to.

The sheriff repeated, "Great." Though from the look on his face things were far from great. "I'm glad for the assist."

If the sheriff of his hometown had *anything* to do with what had happened to Nate and Jennie, Patrick was going to figure it out.

Out the corner of his eye, he saw her take a half step back and glance over. Reacting to his words?

Of course, he was sticking around.

Her eyes were wide with surprise. But why? Obviously he cared about both of them. Nate, more so. There was no sting of betrayal when he looked at the boy. But he didn't want anything happening to either one. Nate needed protection, and he needed his mother with him.

Patrick had no intention of coming between them. Even if he and Jennie had to have a hard conversation about how this could've happened, it wouldn't change what he'd missed out on with Nate. Talking through it would help them get past it. But it wasn't going to get back time.

What was done was done. Now it was all about getting to know Nate and being a good father.

She had to know that.

Patrick said to the sheriff, "I'll send you the location of the house where they were held…"

Johns was already nodding before he even finished. "I'll go there personally and see if I can find anything that will tell us who these guys are."

"I already walked through it once, but I was moving quickly so I might've missed something. Or they could have come back after." His phone buzzed and he looked at the screen. Eric was on his way.

The men could be at the house now. Or they could have cleaned up what was left.

The sheriff might find nothing at all.

Patrick was tempted to thank God that he'd found Jennie, and then her son. That Tucker had caught the scent and Nate was safe in the hospital. But he'd left faith behind as well when he'd left town.

Despite the blessing of now having so much in his life, and it coming so unexpectedly, he couldn't thank God. Not when He was a God that Jennie believed in. She was the one who'd kept the truth from him. Did God really want that from His people?

The sheriff said, "Both of you, come by my office. I'll get you on the computer so you can look at mug shots. All that stuff is digital now."

"I'm not leaving Nate." Jennie took hold of the boy's hand, as though she was about to be dragged from his bedside. Separated from him against her will.

Did she think he hated her that much?

"I can do it," Patrick told her. "But Nate will be here at

least until tomorrow, right? If we make sure he's safe—maybe one of your friends can sit with him—you'll be a help to me. You spent longer with those men."

She got that look in her eyes. The one a witness got before they announced they were refusing to testify and wanted nothing at all to do with the case. Because fear had gotten the best of them.

Patrick said, "My partner will be here tonight. If Nate has a familiar face with him, and there's an officer I trust on the door, could you go with me?"

It was plain in her frown that she didn't like it. "I… Yes. I could do that."

He figured that meant it was possible, though she clearly didn't want to. He couldn't blame her. Patrick hardly wanted to leave Nate's side now that he knew the boy was his son.

He studied the sleeping child, seeing the line of his nose and the set of his eyes. It made him want to cling hard to him and never let go. But what kind of life would that be for either of them?

Patrick stood. "I'm going to walk the sheriff out."

Jennie nodded.

Patrick didn't go far. Just enough that she wouldn't be able to hear the conversation, but he could still see the curtained-off area where she sat with Nate. She probably needed some time alone to be with him. They'd been through an ordeal, and there was a chance it wasn't over yet.

Sheriff Johns squared up on him, chin raised. "Something you need?"

"Any idea who might be behind all this?"

"Trespassers? No. But now a kidnapping?" Johns shrugged. "I guess you'd better ID them."

"And you're fine with state police working a case in

your town?" He'd met more than a few small-town sheriffs. They all had their own way of doing things. And differing opinions on the assistance they'd like from state police.

Except this wasn't assistance. It was Patrick's case now.

"If it keeps them safe, of course." A flash lit the sheriff's eyes. "And you can tell me if she has anything to do with this."

"Excuse me?"

"The daughter of a man who ran the drug trade in this town for *years*." He huffed. "She's either involved, or she knows who is. That's why I called you. So you can use your resources to investigate Jennie's involvement in all this."

SIX

The curtain pulled back. She'd been expecting Patrick again, but it was Beth. Jennie jumped up from the chair as soon as her best friend entered. Relief nearly sent her to her knees. At just a familiar face? Yes, considering this familiar face was the least dramatic person Jennie had ever met.

"Rough night?" Beth probably meant it as a joke, but it didn't sound like she thought it was funny. "I couldn't believe it when I saw the state of your house. I called the sheriff right away." Beth pulled back, her attention on Nate now. "How is he?"

"They gave him something to knock him out. He was pretty stressed. Thanks for coming. He'll need a friend here if he wakes up and I'm not back yet."

"Was that really…him?" Beth wandered over to the bedside.

Jennie nodded. Her friend knew all about Patrick.

"Talk about *whoa.*"

"Yep."

Beth had been new in town when they'd met at the library. Jennie had been there with Nate, around four at the time. They'd instantly clicked. Bonus: Beth hadn't known anything about Jennie's father and his criminal activity. Though she'd told her friend *everything*, which was how she knew about Patrick. Double bonus: Beth had reintroduced her to Jesus Christ and told her how He had saved her.

Jennie had gone to church every Sunday since. Faith was everything to her, and God had showed up time and time again over the years.

Beth frowned. "What is it?"

"I just..." Jennie gathered her thoughts. "I've seen God do so much. Why would I question whether or not He's going to show up, even in this?"

Her friend smiled. "I'm so good at giving counsel, I don't even have to say anything."

Jennie burst out laughing then clapped a hand over her mouth. Her friend gave her another quick squeeze. "Thanks." Jennie blew out a breath. "I needed that."

"After being kidnapped?" Beth shook her head. "I can't believe that happened to you guys. I thought this was supposed to be a safe little town. First, they're trespassing, and then they escalate to kidnapping. I can hardly believe it."

"I'm just glad the sheriff actually called the state police for help."

"And they sent—" Beth glanced at the curtain, then whispered "—Nate's father."

"He knows. Nate was actually the one who said something."

Beth frowned. "Patrick didn't know?"

"He had no idea." Jennie sighed. "Patrick grew up here. It makes sense that the state police sent him."

"And it turns out Nate's dad's a cop. A *handsome* cop."

"Those things will make him a good father?"

Beth said, "You know what I mean."

Yeah, she did. Jennie had to admit the man he'd grown

into wasn't just cute. He was pretty much breathtaking. She had to quit thinking about him. She didn't need the distraction. Not when gunmen had held them—terrorized them—for hours.

Mom!

She could still hear him cry out for her when she'd fallen down that mountainside. Tears filled her eyes.

Beth's warm hand touched hers. "You're both safe now."

Jennie thought about Patrick and the fact that he was there. "No, we're not."

Their lives were in danger. Their hearts were in danger.

Though she had no intention of being vulnerable with Patrick, he still represented a threat.

Jennie squeezed her eyes shut. She heard Beth whispering prayers, covering them both with God's love and protection. That strange dichotomy between what they possessed, by virtue of being God's children, and yet being able to ask for those things in even greater measure—and so much more.

Thank You.

Patrick cleared his throat.

Jennie said, "One second." She kissed her son goodbye and exchanged another hug with her friend.

"Beth's already met my partner." Patrick motioned to the man beside him.

Her friend blushed, but there was no time to decipher that as Patrick continued his introduction.

"This is Officer Eric Fields."

Eric wasn't as tall as Patrick, his features darker. He grinned and stuck out his hand. "You're Jennie."

His whole demeanor caused her guard to slip a little. "I'm afraid so."

He chuckled and they shook hands, though his gaze drifted to the still-open curtain and the spot where Beth sat beside Nate. "I'll watch out for Nate. And your friend in there."

Patrick said, "Eric is going to stand guard until we get back."

Considering the badge and the gun, and the fact the guy put her at ease the way a friend should, she nodded. "Okay." She turned to Patrick. "We won't be gone that long, though. Right?"

"Just long enough to get you and Nate fresh clothes and then swing by the sheriff's office to ID the men who held you."

She figured the quicker they went, the quicker they would get back. Hopefully before Nate even woke up. She was exhausted, but still the reserves to get things done for her son's sake kept her going. Soon enough she would crash, and probably sleep for a couple of days.

Would Patrick stay with Nate while she did that?

Eric said, "Nice to meet you."

"You, too."

Patrick led her away. "Let's go. The quicker we get this done, the quicker we can get back here."

She glanced at him.

"What?"

"Nothing. I agree with you, that's all. I actually thought the same thing a second ago."

"Great minds think alike?"

Did he remember? Years ago, they'd constantly had similar ideas. It had been a pillar of their relationship, that connection. Now, she wasn't so sure. Maybe there was a piece of it still there, but life had taken them in completely different directions. Even if she wanted to salvage something, she wasn't sure there was anything there to work from.

They fell into silence as they made their way outside. Patrick scanned the parking lot, one hand on his gun. Making sure Jennie was safe.

As they approached his SUV, Tucker barked.

"I should take him over to that grass. He's been cooped up for a bit."

She nodded and leaned against the car, watching Patrick walk his dog.

Fatigue weighed on her. Jennie had to fight it off, stomping her feet to keep awake. As a bonus, the movements kept her warm, since she'd given Patrick his jacket back.

Across the lot, a car sat with its engine running. Jennie frowned. The man inside, was he watching her?

"What is it?" Patrick glanced in the direction she was looking while Tucker walked close enough to brush against her leg.

She leaned down to pet the dog's head. "Probably just me being paranoid."

"Maybe."

The car set off and the driver pulled out of the lot.

"Like I said—" Jennie reached for the door handle "—it's probably nothing."

But she wasn't so sure.

When he asked Jennie for directions to her house so he could forgo GPS on his phone, and she gave Patrick the street where she'd lived in high school, all thoughts of that other car disappeared.

His foot let off the gas and he turned to her.

"Yes." The tight tone of her voice matched her body language. "I live in my father's house."

"I'm not passing judgment."

She huffed.

"It's not like you still live with *him*. Right?"

Patrick winced and headed for her place. Probably not the best thing he could have said. Maybe she'd grieved for her father. A lot of people whose parents weren't nice to them, or even good people, still grieved the loss. A bad parent was still a parent. Sometimes they were all a person had.

The house was dark when he pulled onto the lane. Set back from the street, the single-level ranch house had a stucco exterior and red-clay roof tiles.

He parked and glanced over at Jennie. Her eyes were shut, her breathing shallow and steady. He didn't want to wake her but there wasn't much choice. "Hey." He gently shook her shoulder while Tucker sniffed at the open window behind him.

Jennie came awake fast.

"It's okay. It's me."

"Rick?" She glanced around. "Oh. We're here. That felt like five seconds of sleep."

"Sorry. Do you want to take a nap while we're here? Tucker and I can stand guard if you want to rest."

"I don't even want to take the time out to shower." She wrinkled her nose. "But I probably should."

Patrick grabbed his door handle. He didn't need to be distracted by thoughts of how cute she was. The teen girl he'd been so enamored with had grown into a beautiful woman. Too bad he'd abandoned the idea of a relationship. Why be vulnerable again when what they'd had already destroyed him?

"Let me check out the house first. I'd like you to wait by the front door."

"Oh. Okay."

She might not agree, but she did as he'd asked while Patrick gave Tucker the command to roust anyone who might be hiding in the home.

It was a task they'd done a hundred times.

When Tucker returned to him, tail wagging in expectation of his reward, Patrick gave him a rubdown. "Good boy. Yes, you are a good boy."

The dog sat.

Then Tucker raised up to almost shoulder height and snagged the treat from Patrick's fingers. The dog lowered back to stand on all four paws, clearly pleased with himself that he'd earned this unique reward.

Patrick patted his head. "Go play."

"What does that mean?"

He turned to Jennie, who'd shut the front door behind her. "It means we're done with work, and he can just… be a dog." The animal sniffed around, then trotted down the hall. "He's probably looking for Nate, since he knows his scent now."

Jennie trailed down the hall.

Patrick had never been in the house before. The decorations were Southwestern, with lots of color and Mexican tile on the floor. Jennie clearly liked cacti and succulents. Pots of all sizes decorated nearly every surface, even the round dining table.

He found her in the main bedroom, gathering items from her drawers, which she set in a big canvas tote bag. The logo on the side was from Grand Canyon National Park. Patrick found Tucker in Nate's room, sniffing under the bed.

"What did you find, buddy?" He crouched and found a single battered tennis shoe along with two toy dinosaurs. On the wall were posters of zoo animals but the bedspread seemed to be dedicated to his favorite video game.

"I've been looking everywhere for that." Jennie took the shoe from him. "Thanks."

"Tucker is the one who found it."

She rummaged in the closet and came up with a matching shoe. Then she pulled pajamas and clean clothes from the dresser. "I'm surprised Nate can find anything in here."

Patrick grinned. "I'm pretty sure my bedroom looked exactly like this when I was a kid."

He'd been into sports, too, but nature was a passion of his. Animals. Being outside was his preference, and he did it as much as he could—which was fine with Tucker.

Patrick couldn't put into words how it felt to know Nate shared his interests. He knew what they were going to talk about. And what kind of shows they would watch together the first weekend they spent with each other.

The bittersweet pang in his chest shouldn't have been a surprise.

He walked through the rest of the house, despite Tucker's assessment that it was safe and he could relax.

Tucker followed, and Patrick let him out the patio door so he could sniff around there, as well.

Even when he and Jennie had been dating, she'd always come to his house. Mostly when his mom was working— which explained a lot of the trouble they'd gotten into. Being alone with the girl he'd thought he loved had been a heady experience he'd been too immature to realize was risky.

But the result?

He couldn't deny the fact that, without those mistakes, Jennie wouldn't have had Nate. He wouldn't have a son who had suddenly become his whole world. And how was that even possible? He'd gone from not knowing his boy and feeling like he was so alone in the world to having a family. All in one night. Jennie was the girl who had gotten away. Now she would be a part of his life forever, in one way or another.

And Nate would always be his son.

Patrick heard the shower come on. He didn't blame Jennie for wanting to clean up. She'd been kidnapped and injured. She probably wanted to wash off the stress along with the grime of the past day. And it would help to wake her up.

He didn't begrudge her wanting to get back to Nate as quickly as possible, either. Patrick felt the same way.

Ten minutes later she emerged in fresh clothes, her wet hair hanging loose over her shoulders. Patrick slid the patio door open. "Tucker, come!"

He heard the animal's tags jingle before he saw him.

In the distance, multiple sets of headlights flashed across the expanse of land he knew was behind her house.

Patrick stepped outside. He heard Jennie come out after him. She gasped.

"It's them. The trespassers." Fear threaded through her tone. "They're here again."

SEVEN

Jennie needed to get back to her son, not dragged into another kidnapping. The men who'd taken her and Nate had warned her off a few times from "meddling" in what they were up to on her land.

"I'm calling the DEA again." She stepped back inside. "And this time, someone had better call me back."

She was sick of being blown off. Having her instincts questioned, like Johns telling her it was nothing but high school kids. No way. She knew what danger smelled like.

That might sound crazy to some, but she'd been raised in a home with a drug dealer. Her brother hadn't cared one bit. Jennie, on the other hand, had developed an instinct for danger. Grown men in multiple trucks thought they could do whatever they wanted to on her land.

Well, she wasn't going to just stand around and allow her son to be placed in danger. Not again. Where was her phone? She didn't know where she'd put it the last time she—

"Jennie." Patrick snagged her arm and tugged her around until she faced him, shaking her head.

Her breath hitched and only a sob came out. Patrick's expression softened and he pulled her in for a hug. Jennie backed up, shaking her head. "No. Don't." She'd fall apart if he hugged her.

"I'm fine." She wound her arms around her waist.

"You don't have to be."

"It doesn't matter. Nate is the only thing that matters and we need to get back to him." She wiped tears from her face. "After I call the cops."

"Jennie, I am the cops." He pulled out his phone and tapped the screen. "I reported the activity to my lieutenant."

That was it? All her problems solved with a simple message?

Jennie wandered to the hall and grabbed the duffel she'd packed. Her and Nate. Just the two of them. Patrick didn't even care enough to mention the fact she'd made a nice home for her son. He knew the kind of father she'd grown up with. After he'd died, she'd put her heart and soul into this house, redecorating what she had money to do bit by bit. Coloring her walls with leftover paint that the hardware-store owner passed on to her. Yard sales and secondhand-store furniture.

She'd finished it with pillow covers she'd sewn herself. The plants were all in pots she'd made. Experiments and castoffs she couldn't sell. Nate said those were his favorites.

Jennie glanced around the living and dining room. Patrick stood in the center, staring at her. After the shower, she'd put on her favorite shirt, and he hadn't even reacted. He'd loved her when she'd been young and beautiful. Now she was just Nate's mother. A woman he used to know.

"I hated this house when I was growing up."

"I know." Why was he looking at her like that?

She couldn't decipher his expression and there was no point trying. This man was a stranger. "I changed every single thing about it. Even knocked down the wall that used to divide the living room and kitchen, making it open plan."

"You want to talk about renovation right now?"

"No. I want you to know that I made something I'm proud of. A life for our son that has nothing to do with anything associated with my father. Not since he died."

"Okay."

"My brother might've thought what Dad did was cool, but I did *not*. And I don't want it *anywhere near* Nate."

Patrick nodded. "I know you wouldn't put him in danger."

But she had. "I thought I was doing the right thing, calling the sheriff. When he did nothing, it was logical to go up the chain. Call the Feds."

Patrick nodded again. It was like he had no opinion at all. Was this what he did with criminals? Maybe he thought she was lying and this was an interrogation. *Please, Lord.* She didn't want him trying to throw her in jail. Or worse, taking Nate from her.

Dread settled over her. Was that why he was still here?

Patrick glanced at the framed picture over the living room mantel. "Do you have a camera?"

"Yes." She'd taken that picture. Finally, something about her and her life here that he might actually appreciate.

"Get it. We can take pictures of those trucks on your land, get evidence of who they are and show it to the sheriff."

"Are you serious?"

"Quickly, please. We need to catch them in the act." He was looking at her with a soft expression she didn't understand. "You're beyond exhausted, and I'd like to get you back to Nate before I also run out of steam. Otherwise we'll both need sleep right when Nate needs to see one of our faces."

She wanted to make a quip about a son and that special bond they had with their mother. But even "beyond exhausted," she knew that wouldn't be fair to Patrick.

Jennie got her camera. And because she needed help where she would actually get something in return, she also grabbed her Bible. That was the place she should be looking for reassurance and answers. For peace and hope for the future.

Not in Patrick, who'd left once. He'd proved she couldn't trust him. *God, he can't let Nate down. I couldn't bear to watch Nate go through that.* It was the last thing her son needed.

Jennie could withstand a whole lot of hurt. But she knew what it felt like to lose a beloved parent.

It was why she'd done everything she could to make this house a home her mother would have loved. All through the process, she'd told Nate stories of his grandmother, who'd passed away when Jennie was in middle school. Then he'd asked about his father. Why hold back from him? She'd had good memories. Now Nate could make good ones of his own.

She just had to keep herself from getting hurt in the process. As much as she could, at least. That meant holding back any feelings she might have for Patrick. Refusing to give in, even the slightest, to anything that had the potential to grow into what it had once been.

Love she'd never forgotten.

That she could never allow to be again.

Patrick needed to get out of this house. Bright colors, small touches that brought the whole place to life. Including the photo over the mantel, his favorite view in all of

New Mexico. The mountains surrounding their town, where they'd hiked together so many times.

Compared to his apartment in Albuquerque, this house was a home. Somewhere he'd actually want to return to at the end of the day. Instead of the barren rooms where he "lived" that were nothing more than a place to leave his stuff.

Something snagged his attention on a pot on the floor in the corner. He picked it up and rotated it in his hands. The clay was misshapen, but sturdy. It had been painted royal blue with a dusting of yellow over the top half.

"Nate made me keep that one."

"You made it?"

She nodded, her eyes puffy and her face still damp from her tears. He had to look at the pot again, because she was so beautiful it actually hurt to look at her. "It's beautiful."

"I don't know about that. But he wouldn't let me start over. He insisted we fire it, and he painted it himself. Gave it to me for Mother's Day." She sniffed. "He said he learned at church that God takes broken things and makes them beautiful."

Tears blurred Patrick's vision. His mom had said something similar to him once. She still believed it, but he'd never been able to grasp that truth for himself. Life always held him back from believing.

"We should go." He set the pot down and cleared his throat. "Tuck."

The dog trotted in from the kitchen.

"I'm ready." Jennie waved the camera at him.

"We won't interfere. I don't need you in danger, so you won't be anywhere near the line of fire, but I can't leave without taking a look to see if your instincts were right. Then we'll get over to the sheriff's office."

She nodded. "I trust you."

The words settled like lead might in his stomach. He rubbed his abdomen as they stepped out front and she locked the door. "This is a spare key. I have no idea where my purse or my phone are. And my wallet is in my purse, as well."

"You think they were stolen the night you were taken?" He pulled out his phone. "I can have Eric come and change the locks."

A shiver rolled through her. "Why take my purse and phone? Do you think they're going to, like…steal my identity?" Fear was stark on her face.

"We'll find out." He wasn't supposed to make any assurances to the victim. Not when it was a promise he might not be able to keep. But her saying, straight-out, that she trusted him? Patrick wanted to promise a whole lot.

He loaded up Tucker and then sat in the driver's seat with the engine running while he studied the map on his phone.

In the span of a few hours, everything had changed. He wanted to tell her he'd be there for her. Whatever she or Nate needed. Like requesting a transfer and getting a position in this more northern part of New Mexico. A place he'd promised himself he'd never come back to. And now he wanted to live here, as close as possible to Nate. Permanently.

As close as Jennie would let him be.

Patrick cracked the rear windows so Tucker could smell the breeze while he drove. He headed for the main road and then took a dirt track that cut across her land and threaded toward the back of her sixty-some acres. "Anything out here I should be wary of?"

She fiddled with the strap on the camera case in her

lap. "Just a dozen or so cows. Nate doesn't really enjoy the part where they're taken away. I haven't explained to him about hamburger yet. He likes to name them, especially the babies." She said, "I thought about sheep, but this is the *way* wrong climate for them. Doesn't your cousin live in Scotland?"

Patrick nodded. "Yeah. Neil isn't a sheep farmer, though. He's a cop like me, and a K-9 handler with the Edinburgh police. They use Airedales, as well, which is why I got the idea for Tucker. No one believed me that training a terrier would be worth the work it was going to take, but he's more than proved himself over the past six years."

And not just because he had gotten Nate back, to Jennie and him.

"You never left your home. You just made it your own." He didn't know why he'd said that, but it was out now. There was no taking the words back.

"I love my home. And that's not even about it becoming mine at a time when I had nothing. I couldn't afford to move. Not on what I was making back then, going to art school. Trying to raise Nate." She fell quiet for a second. "Still, I'll always think of my mother more than my father when I walk out here. The house is mine and Nate's now. It doesn't remind me of him at all."

The dirt road disappeared beneath the headlights.

Jennie put her hand on his arm. "Slow down a little."

He eased off the gas. "What is it?"

"A wash."

The SUV dipped down and they traversed what he realized would be a river—if it actually rained here. There was no snow, so no runoff. On rare occasions when the weather was wet, this would be a running stream. Right now it was only a dip in the road.

He hit the gas and they climbed up on the far side, bumping over a couple of ruts. If he hit one too fast, it could bend or crack the axle. Should that happen, they would be in serious trouble.

"I'm not sure how close we'll get," he told her. "I'd rather go in with the lights off, but we might run into a hazard and either get stuck or flip over. And if we leave the headlights on, they'll see us."

He slowed to a stop and studied the terrain. The headlights on the far edge of her land were still a ways off.

"This dirt track goes all the way back there, where they are." Her voice trembled. "But I don't think I want to meet them."

"That's probably a wise choice."

He eased the SUV to a stop and then put it in Reverse. Back to the wash, where they went down onto the dry riverbed and up the far side.

As they crested the incline on the other side, he saw lights to his left. "Someone else is out here."

The lights shifted and one pair split off into two pairs. Four beams. But not spaced the way headlights were.

Those were dirt bikes.

He heard the roar of engines cut over the sound of his own and the noise brought with it a tremor of foreboding. "We need to get out of here."

He'd barely finished speaking when automatic gunfire echoed across the night sky, a rapid *crack, crack* of bullets headed right for them.

A stream of shots slammed into the back quarter panel. Patrick gripped the steering wheel and slammed on the gas.

EIGHT

Jennie twisted in her chair to see where the bullet cracked the window. "Tucker!"

"He okay?" Patrick's voice was strained. "Tucker?"

The dog whined, turning around in the back. Nervous. He barked at the roar of engines.

"It's okay, buddy." Jennie hadn't been around dogs all that much. Tucker put his nose to the wire separating the rear of the vehicle from the back seat. Too far for her to reach. "It's okay." She didn't know what else to say.

"How many are there?"

Jennie surveyed the scene behind them. "Four, maybe. I can't see that well." It was pitch-black. The headlights on the dirt bikes dipped and moved so fast she could barely keep track of them. It reminded her of strobe lighting.

She turned back to Patrick, his gaze pinned on his side mirror. He seemed to be waiting for—

Patrick jerked the wheel to the left. The back corner of the SUV clipped one of the bikes. Blasts of gunshots erupted and the headlight flashed as the bike flipped over.

"You got him."

"I know." Patrick had two hands on the wheel. He

seemed to know what he was doing. The confident, capable police officer. But that didn't remove the danger.

There were three more. "I can't believe they're running around like this on my land."

The bikes kept chase.

Patrick said nothing, driving steady. Checking his mirrors every few seconds. "Herding us."

"Off *my* land." Hot anger boiled in her stomach. How many times had she called Sheriff Johns and he'd said it was nothing but teenagers?

That wasn't what this was.

These were adults who thought they could do whatever they wanted on *her* land.

"I'm not leaving. They're the ones who don't belong here." Three bikes pursued them. "They're not trying to kidnap me again. They're up to something here, right? They don't want me to see what it is." She folded her arms and huffed out a breath. "I'm not just going to be some helpless victim."

Not only had she not been raised that way, Jennie wasn't raising Nate that way. Her son needed to know how to be both strong *and* kind. It was rare to find someone who possessed both qualities.

"I know." Patrick's tone was a cross between someone trying to placate a crazy person and someone resigned to a situation they couldn't control. "But that doesn't mean this is the time to fight back."

Excuse me? "You want me to just sit here?"

"Honestly? Yes." He sighed. "I don't want any of us getting hurt by these guys. Right now, they're leaving us alone. If we can get out of here without any more gunshots aimed at us, that's the best scenario. They're letting us leave. See?"

Jennie studied the dirt biker out the left back window. The one on her side had a huge semiautomatic gun strapped across his back.

Stalemate? Was that what this was? She wanted these men—and the ones who had kidnapped her—to pay for the fear now running through her veins. She was flushed, sweating and freezing at the same time. Like her body didn't know what to do.

She never wanted Nate to experience this. Not before, when they'd been in that house, and not ever again.

A whimper left her throat. Patrick reached over and took her hand. He squeezed it, then held it, resting on her knee. "It's going to be okay. They're leaving us alone, and we're almost at the road."

True to his word, they bumped up onto the blacktop. Patrick turned toward the center of town.

"Now we go see the sheriff."

Jennie checked behind them. As they drove away, the three bikers sat at the end of the dirt track—no, there were only two now. Had one gone back, concerned for their friend? They were bad guys. They probably cared about nothing. Except money and the power they wielded over people they considered to be weaker.

"What do they want with *my* land? There's nothing special about it, except that it's just land."

Patrick was quiet long enough she wondered if he would say anything. The second he did, she knew she'd rather he hadn't. "Didn't you say your father had used the back forty to transport drugs across the state?"

"And what would that have to do with me now? It's been years." She was glad he'd let go of her hand for the bump onto the blacktop. She didn't want to hold it ever again. Not if he thought for one second that she would bring drugs into her son's life.

It was because she'd been determined to keep those

things far from Nate that they'd ended up in this situation in the first place. Trying to do the right thing. That's what had led to the kidnapping.

She kind of wished she'd been there long enough to meet the boss, as she dearly wanted the chance to spit in his face.

Patrick thinks I'm involved.

He knew how she'd felt about drugs. Selling them, trafficking them. It didn't matter where someone was in the chain, it was *wrong.* The people who supplied that stuff preyed on the vulnerable. She didn't want to be around any of that, and there was no way she'd let it near Nate.

He should know she would never do that. Right? But the truth was, they didn't know each other.

Not anymore.

Patrick mulled over everything on the way to the sheriff's office while Jennie's ire bled away next to him. He knew she was scared. He hadn't expected the anger. She was a force to be reckoned with. A strong woman passionate about keeping her son safe—and she was willing to put her life on the line to do it.

No matter how far they moved on from the past, Patrick would always be aware of what he'd lost.

Could he forgive her?

That would be contingent on her allowing him all the way into their family. He didn't want to muddy things. Once he'd ensured they were safe, he wanted time to get to know his son.

Right now what he needed was information. That was why he didn't delay ushering her inside the sheriff's office. They could have talked in his vehicle, but why be alone and chance getting sucked further into thinking about her?

He should be doing his job.

"Sheriff." Patrick got his attention and explained what had happened at her house.

Johns lumbered to a side office and leaned in. "Melanie, be a doll and send Ted over to Ms. Wilson's ranch. Tell him to be careful."

"Copy that, Sheriff."

Then he crossed over to a desk and waved them over. "Let's get you all set up here." He jiggled the mouse on an ancient-looking computer and then pecked with two fingers to bring up the database.

"You sit. I need to talk to the sheriff," Patrick said.

Jennie glanced at him but didn't argue.

As she looked through the mug shots in the county database, Patrick motioned for Johns to join him out of her earshot.

"What is it, son?"

I'm not your son. Patrick didn't remind him that it was "Officer Sanders" even though he wanted to. "This seems to be personal to Ms. Wilson. Do you have any idea why that might be?"

This sheriff had been in the job for nearly twenty years now, according to the news article framed on the wall. He had to have known Jennie's father. After all, he'd insinuated she might be involved in all this.

What Johns didn't seem to know was Patrick's personal connection to Nate—and it was none of the man's business. Patrick had no intention of giving the sheriff ammunition to have him pushed aside on this case.

He was all in, until Nate and Jennie were safe.

The sheriff glanced from Jennie back to Patrick. "Have you asked her that?"

"I wanted your take first. As the law in this town, you must have an idea who's behind the trespassing. And I know you don't believe it's just kids."

"We'll see what's what when my deputy reports in."

"A bit risky, don't you think, sending someone out there alone? This Ted person, whoever he is, sticking his neck out. You need to send more men before something bad happens."

"It's as risky as taking a civilian into an unknown situation."

Patrick knew then he wouldn't get far calling this man out. He might be a decent sheriff, but he was also stubborn and prideful.

"What information I choose to disseminate to those private citizens in my care is up to me," Johns said. "And scaring a young single mom isn't how I operate."

"You don't think she should exercise caution? You blew her off and she called the DEA."

"Which put her in more danger." The sheriff huffed. "I told her to be careful, and that didn't mean calling in a bunch of cowboy Feds. We both know how quick they are to shoot first, with no intention of asking any questions later."

Patrick shrugged. "What's done is done. The issue here is what will happen going forward. I've got my partner in the mix, but he's watching out for Nate—which is what I intend to do as soon as Jennie has identified those men. What I'd like to know is what you plan to do."

If something needed doing that wasn't being done, Patrick would move in regardless of the sheriff's wants.

The men who'd taken Jennie and Nate and held them at gunpoint, scared for their lives, would be locked in a jail cell as soon as Patrick located them.

"Put a name to the faces, and I'll go round them up."

Patrick pressed his lips together. There wasn't much point belaboring anything with a sheriff who wanted to do things single-handedly.

Could there really be a drug operation in town, akin to what Jennie's father had accomplished? If there was, Sheriff Johns probably wasn't as in the dark as he pretended. Just to save face? Patrick wasn't sure about that. He was probably used to politicking. Holding things close to his vest and then disseminating information in a way that kept his position and respect in town. If it seemed like he was having trouble maintaining order, it probably wouldn't play well for the next election.

Was he planning on running again soon? That would explain him downplaying drug-trafficking across land belonging to a private citizen.

"Hey."

Patrick pulled a chair up to the desk where Jennie sat. "Hey. You okay?"

"I haven't found anything, if that's what you mean."

"Partly. But I also want to know if you're hanging in there."

Jennie blew out a breath and refocused on the monitor. "I'll be better when I'm back with Nate."

"Me, too."

They shared a smile. Patrick wondered if it would be the first of many, or if things between them would always be tense.

Jennie gasped. "That's one. I found one."

Patrick yelled, "Sheriff!"

She jumped.

"Sorry." Patrick looked at the picture. A man he hadn't had a clear view of in the dark. "Click that."

Jennie tapped the mouse button.

He raised his eyebrows at the name Carl Andrews. "Wasn't he friends with your brother?"

NINE

"My brother?" Jennie turned, aware of the frown on her face. Given the last day or so, she figured she looked like a recently showered person…who had been through the ringer. Scared for her life. Running across a mountain. Falling down said mountain.

Not exactly date-night ready. But then, she hadn't done that in so long she probably had no hope.

Maybe in another ten years, when Nate was out of the house, she would find a nice man. Settle down. Though, when she pictured that dream, it was Patrick standing on her doorstep with flowers, ready to take her out.

Cue another frown.

"Ms. Wilson."

She blinked and glanced at the sheriff. "I'm sorry… what was that?"

"I asked when the last time you saw your brother was."

How did she even begin to count that? Years. More than a decade. "Longer than the last time I saw Patrick." She saw him wince but kept her attention on the sheriff. "Martin left for the army right out of high school, and he's three years older than me. So it's been a long time."

"He never came back to visit?"

"I called him when my father died," she said. "He never even came back for the funeral."

"Wow." Patrick shook his head. "I remember him being a piece of work, but that takes the cake. The army surprises me, though. He got in so much trouble in high school I'm surprised he managed to have a career in the military."

"I always figured he either straightened up his life and just didn't want anything to do with home or family. Or he dropped out of the army, maybe even ended up in jail again, and still didn't want anything to do with home or family."

Either outcome, same thing. It meant she had no brother in her life. And considering how Martin had treated her—and the things she was pretty sure he'd done for their father back then—she figured that was no loss. Nate didn't need an uncle like that in his life.

"This isn't anything to do with my brother. He hasn't come back to town, right? Or he'd have probably come asking for money." She didn't know how much more plainly to say it. "Carl Andrews and whoever his associate is work for someone. But it has nothing to do with Martin. I can assure you of that."

"Okay." Patrick nodded. "Sheriff, do you know this Carl Andrews? If we have an idea who his associates are, or where we might find him, we'll be closer to bringing him in."

While they talked, Jennie scrolled through the mug shots to try to find the second man. There might be a way for her to look at Andrews's known associates in the police database, if the sheriff had them connected in this system.

She didn't know if that function was even part of this computer program, but it was possible. She'd put together her own database of customers she sold to directly through her website, as well as stores she sold to on consignment. So how hard could it be to find a box to click in this program?

Her thoughts drifted back to her brother. Why? She'd meant what she'd said about this having nothing to do with him. Was that because she didn't want to believe Martin would do something like that to her? Maybe he was angry that she'd inherited everything.

But it wasn't like that was her fault. When the will had been read, she'd found out that the house and all the property, which had been in her mother's name, had been left to her. She hadn't believed it, either. All their father's death had done was pass ownership of everything officially to Jennie. She hadn't even known that her father had withheld that information from her. The land had belonged to her grandfather—her mom's dad. Her father hadn't owned any of it.

Because he hadn't wanted the authorities to be able to seize anything?

Jennie had made it her own. Her father was deceased. There was no point in being angry with him for keeping her home for himself. If he hadn't died from that heart attack, would she ever have discovered the truth?

Jennie studied the photo on the screen. *Not him.* She clicked to the next one and shook off the thoughts that had crowded in her mind.

"Rick." She realized what she'd said and turned. "Patrick." Of course, that was what she'd meant.

He broke off his conversation with the sheriff about BOLOs, whatever those were. "Yes?"

"I found the second man." She got up just for the sake of moving, paced a few steps and turned.

Patrick and the sheriff both stared at the screen. Patrick said, "Michael Danes." He clicked the mouse. "He and Andrews have priors for assault and illegal weapons possession."

Jennie was ready to be done with this whole ordeal. Sheriff Johns and Patrick were both cops. They could take care of Carl Andrews and Michael Danes while she went back to her son and her work. Life would return to normal, but now her son had a father in his life and Jennie had gained the added peace of mind of a cop hanging around the house.

And given what had happened during the past twenty-four hours, he could stay for as long as he wanted. She was ready to feel safe again.

So long as her heart stayed safe, also.

Johns turned to her. "Do you remember either of these guys?"

"Of course. They were the ones who held us in that house." She swung an arm in Patrick's direction. "And they shot at all of us."

"That's not what I mean," Johns said. "Did they work for your father?"

She blinked. Not the question she thought he would have asked her. "How would I know that? It isn't like I was part of his business."

"Maybe you could think back. I know he's been dead a while, but these men might be his associates."

"What would it matter if they were? Like you said, he's been dead a while. Which means that has nothing to do with this—" she pointed at the floor "—what's happening right now, that's putting my son in danger. And you need to do something about it."

"If you were worried about putting your son in danger, then perhaps you shouldn't have gotten involved in the first place," the sheriff shot back.

Patrick started to butt in.

Jennie didn't let him. "I didn't invite them over for dinner. These men dragged me from my house. It's your job to arrest them."

"I'm just glad your actions didn't get your boy killed." Johns shook his head and huffed. "Calling in the DEA. I don't know what you hoped to achieve with that."

Patrick turned to the sheriff. The move put him shoulder to shoulder with Jennie. It occurred to him that it was the two of them now facing off against the sheriff. Not two cops and a civilian. Just Patrick and Jennie, together, as though the rest of the world was on the opposite side.

He had no time to think about how often they'd done that before. Mostly against her father, or teachers who came down on her for being a criminal's daughter, as though her parentage was her fault.

Patrick said, "Now that we've identified the two men, it's time for us to go back to the hospital. I need to check in with my partner, and Jennie wants to see her son."

He left out the part about Nate also being his son. It was still none of the sheriff's business.

Johns held up his hands. "I still need statements from both of you, full written accounts of what happened out there tonight. At the house where you were held, and at your house, Ms. Wilson. So why don't you both take seats and I'll get you some coffee while you write it all down."

Patrick glanced at Tucker, lying in the corner with his chin on his paws. Eyes open, trained on him. He looked about as ready to get out of there as Patrick was.

He checked his phone. "I suppose we can get the paperwork done real quick before we go." When Jennie turned to him, he said, "I'm sure Nate won't wake up until early morning. Isn't that what the doctor said?"

She pressed her lips together and nodded. About as happy to be there as the dog.

"But we won't be having any more cracks about the Feds, okay?" He stared down the sheriff. "What's done was done, and Ms. Wilson did what she thought was best after the *sheriff's department* failed to aid her. Everyone has the right to feel safe in their own home."

"I've been out on her land," Johns said. "All I saw was tire tracks."

"Yes. Because there were vehicles on my land." She lifted her chin. "Ones that didn't belong to me and did not have my permission to be there. Whether you found anything or not, that doesn't mean there wasn't anyone out there."

"I never said you were making it up."

"No, but it seems to me you were supposed to take care of it. You didn't, and my son had a *gun* waved at him. Because he was *kidnapped*."

She strode to the water cooler and stood staring at the wall for a minute, breathing hard.

"This may need to be a federal case." Patrick folded his arms. "Or, at the least, that it's now an investigation that will be undertaken by the state police."

The sheriff started to object. Probably more bluster.

Patrick said, "After all, you have a huge county to patrol and I'd guess not nearly the staff to keep everyone who lives in it safe at all times."

"You try doing my job."

To his credit, the sheriff did have the decency to look guilty that Jennie and Nate had been hurt. Still, as far as Patrick was concerned, if he was going to continue doing things "his way," he'd have to accept the fact that Patrick would find it suspicious they hadn't been able to leave yet. And that Jennie had essentially been blown off.

Whether that was because the sheriff hadn't had time to look more deeply into her concerns—and hadn't known they would escalate to kidnapping—or for nefarious reasons, Patrick didn't know.

He needed to make the guy think everything was fine. Patrick grinned. "I don't know if I'd like it. Would I be able to bring Tucker?" He waved at the dog, who lifted his head after hearing his name.

The sheriff glanced at him, then back at Patrick. "Depends. Can he flush out those guys?"

"Yes. If you know where they're holed up."

Johns's eyes widened.

"It's part of his training."

"I thought he just found missing people, like he did with Nate."

Patrick shrugged. "He's had a lot of different training. You'd be surprised what he can do." He was intensely proud of his dog and the fact that Tucker had proved himself over and over again. Yes, that was mostly because he'd been forced to do so. Not many had believed an Airedale could do this job, despite the fact other police departments used them and had since World War I.

Some people didn't like change.

Patrick studied the sheriff as he situated Jennie with a piece of paper and a pen to write out her statement.

Patrick probably would've said he himself was one of those people set in their ways. At least until his entire life had been upended. He would say the sheriff was likely one of those people, too. There were a lot of cops who'd been doing the job for years and did that job even better with twenty or thirty years under their belt. Then there were the ones who'd be doing the department a favor if they put in for retirement.

He knew which one he'd prefer the sheriff here was.

Especially considering how he'd likely get in the way as they worked to locate the two men Jennie had identified. The sheriff could cause them a whole host of problems.

Perhaps the man would be content to stick in his office and not mind that it was Patrick and his partner who found Carl Andrews and Michael Danes. Perhaps not.

Patrick's phone rang and he pulled it from his pocket. The screen showed his partner's last name: Fields. He swiped and put the phone to his ear. "Sanders."

Jennie looked over. He mouthed *partner* and she went back to writing. Fast. Maybe as fast as she could so they could get out of there.

"You there, bro?" Eric asked.

Patrick turned away from her. "Yeah, I'm here. Everything good?"

"This middle-of-nowhere desert is really where you grew up? I mean, there are some seriously beautiful ladies out here." He cleared his throat.

"That's Jennie's friend."

"Yeah, her, too," Eric said. "Can't believe you grew up here."

"Keep your focus, okay? This isn't something I need you distracted on."

"Hundred percent, bro. I'm paying attention to the kid. You know, the one with your nose, who I still cannot believe is your son. She really kept it from you? She seemed so nice, and you tell me she's this…what? A bold-faced liar?"

Patrick moved out of earshot, but where he could still see Jennie. "She's not a liar. And yes, I told you he's my son."

"Does Tucker like him?"

Patrick thought back to the dog's reaction to his son. "Yes."

"Good enough for me. He's a way better judge of character than you."

Patrick frowned. "Will you focus?"

"Bro—"

"Pay attention. They were kidnapped yesterday, so you need to be vigilant. Whoever wanted to talk to Nate might come back and try to get to him again."

"I know that. I also…"

"Eric. What is it?"

"Yeah, Mom. I know that." Eric paused. "I am taking all my vitamins, Mom. I promise."

"Is someone there?" Not just a person his partner didn't want overhearing his side of a police conversation. Someone else. Someone who would present a threat to Nate.

A bad guy.

Eric said, "Yes. You are always right." The tone was the same, but his meaning was clear.

"Are they on approach to Nate's bed?"

"Yes, Mom. It's true." He chuckled. Not good, since the laugh sounded completely fake.

Someone was trying to reach his son's bed. "I'll be there in five minutes. Don't let *anything* happen to Nate."

TEN

Jennie flung the door open before he'd even shoved the SUV into Park. Tucker barked at her as she jumped out, but she wasn't going to stop for anything.

Someone had approached her son's bay in the hospital.

That cop—Eric. The one Patrick introduced as his partner. He'd been on the phone with Patrick when he'd led him to believe someone was approaching.

That was all she knew.

The whole drive over—which felt like an hour but was closer to a few minutes—she'd asked and asked what was happening with Nate. Never mind that he didn't know more than what he'd already told her. Wasn't withholding anything. Patrick had no intention of keeping her in the dark about what was happening to their son. He just hadn't had more information to give her.

"Jennie!"

She heard him race after her, along with the jingle of Tucker's tags, but just kept going. All the way to the alarmed Emergency room doors. How had someone gotten past them anyway?

Patrick touched the small of her back. She didn't look at him. Not when he did that, and not a second later when the doors slid open. Released by the staff member behind the desk.

Jennie darted between the doors, but Patrick caught her elbow.

Jennie said, "No."

He tugged her around to him, his other hand holding the leash with Tucker close to his side. The dog looked ready to work. "Jennie."

"Nate—"

He cut her off. "You stay behind me." She heard the snick as he drew his weapon. "We don't know who is there. So we're going to let Tucker go first."

She was right behind him, though. No way would she allow anyone to get to Nate if she could help it. But he was correct that he should be the person in front. He had a gun, after all. And that badge on his belt. Tucker sniffed at the floor tiles as they raced down the hall to the bay where he'd been admitted overnight.

She looked around Patrick, but the man she'd met wasn't there. Patrick's partner had worn similar clothes, but now he was gone. A white paper cup lay on the floor, tipped over, its contents spilled in front of the curtain.

Patrick swiped back the curtain, gun raised. Tucker sniffed.

Beth sucked in a breath and blinked away a sleepy glaze in her eyes. Nate lay in the bed, still asleep. Jennie rushed around Patrick and went to her friend, so she didn't disturb her son from his rest.

Beth yawned. "What's going on? I heard someone yell, didn't I?" She looked around Jennie and Patrick. "Where's the other cop?"

"I'm going to find out," Patrick said.

Jennie glanced at him and nodded. Beyond him, a security guard moved into the hall.

"Stay here, watch them and *don't move*," Patrick ordered.

The man seemed a little perturbed but nodded. She didn't know how much help he would be. He had a badge, but only a stun gun on his belt.

Patrick left the man watching over them while he disappeared with Tucker to search for the threat.

"What's going on?"

Jennie looked at Beth. "Patrick was on the phone with his partner, who thought that someone was making an approach."

At least, that was how he'd worded it. But he hadn't known. And where was Eric, anyway? Had he run off after someone? That meant the person hadn't gotten near this hospital bed. Right?

"He needs to find Eric and figure out what happened." Jennie checked on Nate, smoothing down covers that didn't need to be adjusted and laying a soft kiss on his forehead. One he would have groaned about if he'd been awake.

"Oh." Beth rubbed at her eyes.

Jennie glanced at the security guard, who watched them in a kind of detached way while he chatted to the nurse. Of course, he was just a security guard, but she figured Patrick wouldn't have liked it. Still, this man wasn't doing anything she should worry about.

She was just on edge, being paranoid and seeing danger where there was none. Because Patrick was facing down the danger.

And that meant *he* was the one at risk right now.

Something that might be okay with him. But that didn't sit right with her. No matter that he was a cop, she didn't love the idea that he was in the line of fire.

For her, or for anyone else. Maybe that was irrational. Or silly. Either way, it was how she felt.

The security guard glanced down the hall where Patrick had gone. Jennie peeked around the curtain.

She immediately saw the tension between Patrick and his partner. Even Tucker seemed to be on edge. Or just hyperalert.

Jennie raced over. "What happened?"

Eric ended their stare-down and looked at her. "I saw a guy. He clocked me and broke off his approach, so I followed."

"And lost him." Patrick lifted his chin.

"Back off. *Partner.*"

Patrick blew out a breath that sounded like it might've been a huff of laughter but didn't say anything. Jennie wanted to squeeze his arm—something—but given his body language figured he didn't want to be touched right now.

"You saw someone?"

Eric nodded.

She turned to Patrick. "Maybe it was one of those guys I picked out."

"If we look at the surveillance, you can see for yourself. I'm sure he's on the footage." Eric pointed high on the wall to a surveillance camera.

Jennie looked up. On the bottom of the round lens, a red light flashed. Did that mean it was recording?

She glanced at the security guard, who was still watching her son, then turned back.

Patrick hadn't taken his attention from his partner. "You didn't catch him."

"Hard to do that when he clocked the shield from twenty feet away." Eric motioned to the badge on his belt. "He was two floors down the stairwell by the time

I got through the door. No point chasing him when that left the kid exposed."

A muscle in Patrick's jaw flexed.

"Nate is still sleeping," Jennie assured him. "He didn't even wake up." She moved to Tucker and petted him. Maybe if he relaxed, Patrick would, as well.

He turned to her.

"Everything is fine."

"Nate is being targeted," Patrick said. "He's in danger here, the same as he was at your house. We need a safe place to take him."

She nodded. "Okay. Wherever we need to go, we'll go. As long as you and Tucker are with us."

Jennie saw Eric's glance between them. She wanted his friend to think she was a good woman for Patrick's son to have in his life. That she could stand strong and not fall apart at the slightest thing. He didn't need to be saddled with all the work unraveling what was happening and keeping them safe while they did nothing to aid that.

She wasn't going to be deadweight. Some helpless female who couldn't do anything to combat what life threw at her. Together, they would protect Nate.

Patrick turned to her. "I will keep you both safe."

"I know." Her words softened his gaze. He appreciated her faith in him. "You won't let anything happen to Nate."

"To either of you."

She nodded. "Okay."

Okay. So much faith in him. Too bad he didn't have faith in himself.

"She's quite a woman."

Patrick turned back to his partner. "You and I are going to have serious problems if anything like that happens again."

"You think I should have been in two places at once, protecting the kid—who is fine, by the way—and catching the guy who tried to approach?"

Patrick clenched his teeth. He didn't have a better idea for what Eric should have done. In fact, Patrick would likely have done exactly the same thing for the chance to catch whomever it was that had tried to get to Nate.

"I get this is personal," Eric said. "You've never indicated you'd have compromised judgment when it's personal, and I doubt you will. But I'm here to be a sounding board, okay? If you need impartial judgment."

"What I need is a safe place to take Jennie and Nate when they release him. Somewhere they can lay low and actually rest, and I can know they're safe while we find these guys and figure out who's behind this."

"Now you want my help again?"

Patrick nodded. "I need it."

They were partners. Eric was right. This was personal—in a way that was unprecedented. And like every other difference between them, they would work their way past it. At the core, they were two cops. Despite personal differences, they'd been trained the same way and had the same goals.

"Okay, then," Eric said. For them, it was basically an apology. Things were good now and they would move on. "I'll get you a copy of the surveillance footage. See if there's a good angle on this guy's face."

Patrick held his hand out. "I appreciate it."

Eric shook with him, then went to the elevator while Patrick returned to Jennie and Nate. They were like a tether. He didn't want to be too far from either of them. Not for long, at least. Just enough time to figure out what was going on.

Beth stood. "I'm going to go get some coffee. Do either of you need anything?"

Patrick shook his head.

"No, but thanks." Jennie gave her friend a smile.

He took the empty chair and Jennie leaned one hip on the bed in front of him, angled toward Nate. He gave Tucker a command to lie down beside his chair.

Tucker leaned his chin on the bed and Patrick heard him sniffing. Only after he'd done that did Tucker lay down.

Jennie smiled at him. Patrick was tired enough to want to stare at her and not care that she'd see him do it.

He tipped his head to the side. "How are you doing?"

"I feel about as tired as you look."

He felt his lips twitch. "So pretty good, then?"

She smiled back. "I'm not fielding that one. Hit me with another."

"I told Eric we need a safe place to say when Nate is released."

"I don't want to stay here long, but I know he needs medical attention. If the doctor thinks he should be in the hospital then I won't argue." She traced her thumb on the back of Nate's hand. "Even though I have to admit, all this makes me want to gather him up, run away and hide."

"That's understandable," he said. "You want to keep him safe."

Didn't all parents want to safeguard their children? But it was impossible to protect them from everyone and everything that might harm them.

Jennie said, "That's not the best for him, though. He can't live life tucked away from the world. He'll never learn to be strong that way."

"It's still okay to want to protect him. You should want that." He was finding he wanted it, also. Not just because

Nate was vulnerable and in danger. Eric was right about this becoming personal. Patrick could do his job perfectly fine even when the victim was someone he cared deeply about. He'd be inclined to pray just to cover his bases, but that didn't really mean he had faith.

"Jennie?"

"Yes?"

"Will you pray, please? I'd like to know we're covered, but I don't want to be a hypocrite." He needed to admit where he stood with that. "I haven't gone to church in years."

"Because of me?"

"I didn't leave because of you. It was your father who forced my mother and me from our home, and when I went to talk to him…to confront him…a couple of his guys laid into me. They tossed me on the street."

She gasped.

"It was a long time ago. He's not here anymore, which means he can't answer for what he did." Patrick wasn't going to tell her that being kicked so hard two of his ribs had broken wasn't a big deal, because it was. But not as bad as her father trying to toss money at him to induce him to leave Jennie—and town. When he hadn't taken it, they'd attacked him. "Soon as I got home, my mom drove us out of town. I wrote to you in the car."

A tear rolled down her cheek and she wiped it away. She was quiet for a while then said, "He told me he talked to you. That he told you about the baby, and you didn't want to know. That you asked him for money. Then you were just gone." She sniffed. "I went to your house, but you'd already cleared out and left."

Patrick tugged her up and wrapped his arms around her. Jennie melted against him, her arms sliding around his middle as they held each other. He exhaled a long breath, his cheek against her hair.

Patrick studied Nate as he slept. Eyelashes fanned on his cheeks, his chest slowly rising and falling. Together, they'd made him. Though not under the best of circumstances—understatement—it could not be denied that Nate was astounding. Patrick couldn't wait to get to know his son better.

"Oh. Sorry."

Jennie backed away. "It's okay, Beth."

Patrick turned, cold from the loss of her embrace. And from a simple hug? It made no sense, except that it had been a long time and what they'd had was one of those once-in-a-lifetime things.

Eric stood behind Beth.

"What is it?" Patrick lifted his chin.

His partner crowded in, weaving around Beth as they both said, "Sorry. Excuse me." There was hardly enough space for the four of them and the dog, plus the hospital bed where his son lay.

Eric's countenance didn't allow for argument. Especially when he held out his phone. "The security guard sent the email to you, as well."

Patrick looked at Eric's phone screen. The photo was a grainy shot of the hallway. "Can we get an ID from it, see if it's either Carl Andrews or Michael Danes?"

It might also be the boss, who'd wanted to talk to Nate and hadn't cared about Jennie. Who did that? What more value could a child be than his mother? It didn't make sense that they would want him and not her. Patrick needed to figure out this mess.

Before it got worse.

When he looked up, Eric's attention was on Jennie. Why was he…?

Patrick caught the expression on her face.

"Jennie, do you know who that is?"

ELEVEN

Jennie strode between Beth and Eric, out to the hallway, though it wasn't any less crowded than it had been in Nate's bay. She could hardly believe he was still sleeping. But that was due to whatever the doctor had given him.

"Jennie."

She lifted her arms as though they could hide her face from the world and paced away from where Patrick stood. More attempts at avoidance? *No*. Jennie was going to face her problems head-on. She'd survived so much in the last day and a half. She wasn't giving up now.

She took a couple of deep breaths and then lowered her arms.

"You know who it is." Not a question.

"My brother."

She sank into a chair and covered her face again. Patrick tugged her hands down and she saw him crouched in front of her. Tucker got up and sniffed at his face. Patrick nudged him away and said, "The man on the surveillance video, the one who approached Nate's room, was your brother?"

She nodded.

"How can you know that? It's been years since you've seen Martin."

So she was either lying or she was guessing? Jennie didn't know which was worse. "It's him. I know it is."

"The image is grainy." He glanced at the photo on the phone. "I guess it might resemble him."

She sat back in the chair and tugged her hands from his. It didn't matter that Patrick didn't believe her. The picture was of her brother. And now that she thought about it, the whole thing made sense. Not hurting them. Wanting to see Nate.

But Martin was in the army. This had been going on for weeks. Longer than any leave he'd have, right? She hadn't seen her brother since he'd left and didn't know much about army life. But she figured he couldn't just leave his job—or posting—or whatever, and come home for weeks at a time.

"Maybe he's done with the army."

"But he hasn't tried to contact you."

She shook her head. "I have no idea why. If he has, I didn't know it was him."

"What is it about that picture that makes you think it's Martin?"

"The fact I know my brother?"

"Is that a question?" When she didn't answer him, Patrick said, "I knew your brother in high school. He was three years older, but I remember what he looked like then. But this guy?" He shook his head. "I can't say for sure."

"My dad had pictures of him in uniform. I think Martin sent them to him. I have them in a drawer somewhere, so I could show Nate. But I never have."

"And you think that man is Martin?"

"Yes, I do."

He didn't believe her, though, did he? And that hurt a lot. Jennie had been getting used to having Patrick here, supporting her. Helping. It had been a matter of hours, but that was evidently enough time to become dependent on another person. Not just because they'd been in danger, but because she hadn't been alone as a parent anymore.

Now Martin was back?

Instead of coming to the house and ringing the doorbell like anyone else, Martin was involved in something that included trespassing on her land. Then he'd had them kidnapped, and now he was threatening Nate's life?

"I don't want him coming anywhere near me." She stood, lifting her chin as Patrick stood, as well.

Beth had gone back to Nate's bedside, something Jennie would be forever grateful for. Eric stayed at the curtain, another man determined to protect them. But there was nothing in her appreciation for him that even came close to how she felt about Patrick.

That just meant this man in front of her, Jennie's son's father, had the ultimate power over her. Him doubting her identification of that man showed he had the ability to hurt her.

It had crushed her the day she had realized he'd completely cleared out and left her alone—and pregnant— still living in her father's house. Even now, he had the ability to destroy her.

And if she continued to let him into her life, and her heart, that would only get worse.

Until the day he wrecked her all over again. When he inevitably fought her for custody of Nate. He was a cop, while her family was nothing but criminals. There was no way she would win.

Patrick frowned. He looked about to say something when Eric broke in. "It's Martin Wilson?"

Patrick turned to his partner. Jennie exhaled, glad to be relieved from his scrutiny.

"That's what we believe."

Now he believed her? Jennie chose to just be grateful he no longer had that knowing stare aimed at her. The one she figured could see past what she was saying to her deeper feelings. Desperation. Fear.

Both *totally* attractive things. Not.

She wasn't interested in attraction. She didn't need any of that—especially not from a man who had hurt her so deeply in the past. Sure, he would no doubt be a good father to Nate. But that didn't mean he would stick around for Jennie. Literally or figuratively.

There was just too much pain in their history. Miscommunication or not, it would always be between them.

"Let's find out what we can from the army."

Eric nodded.

"Once we have that, we'll be a step closer to figuring out what's going on here."

"Ms. Wilson?"

She turned to find the doctor standing there. "When is Nate able to be released?"

Ready to get back to her normal life, she wanted to take him somewhere they could both rest.

"We'll have to see how he's doing when he wakes up, but it's possible he can go home later today."

Jennie crossed her arms in front of her, trying not to be cynical about doctors or hospitals. She needed to let him do his job. Her fingers grazed across the bandage on her elbow and she winced. "Thank you, Doctor."

Patrick stepped around her and questioned the doctor about things to watch out for with Nate and when he might need to be brought back in.

She turned away, trying to tamp down the frustration. *He's being a good dad, remember?* Plus he was new at this, and cops tended to take charge of situations. She had to repeat the question in her mind four times.

Jennie strode past Nate, glancing over to make sure he was all right. Still sleeping. Beth had her gaze on the other police officer—the one down the hallway. Eric paced, the phone clutched to his ear. She assumed he was asking the army about her brother or talking to his boss.

"Hey." Patrick touched her shoulder. "It's good news that Nate might be released. Right? Are you okay?"

Jennie didn't have the mental energy for a deep conversation. "I'm going to stay by Nate. Please let me know when we're leaving." She went to sit with her son.

She'd done everything she could to have a different life than the one she'd had growing up. Her father had never included her in his "business," but she'd seen enough. That kind of stain spread, and she'd felt its cloying stickiness on her too many times.

That life wasn't something she wanted anywhere near Nate. Not when he'd been born, not now and not ever.

No matter what her brother tried to do.

Fear for his son clouded out everything. Patrick knew exactly how Jennie had felt when she walked out of the bay where Nate slept. That need for space, emotional and physical. A much-needed second in the middle of all that was going on to just take a moment and process.

He had a son.

That son was in danger.

Tucker whined, leaning his body against the side of Patrick's leg. He reached down and patted the dog's head.

Now they knew it was Martin Wilson. But did they? Sure, Jennie's brother might be the man who had come onto this hospital floor to see his nephew. A child he'd never met.

That didn't mean he was the person behind their kidnapping, or whatever was going on with the trespassers on her land.

Patrick didn't think it was a coincidence. The son of a man who'd been the local drug dealer—kingpin, maybe—for years, strong-arming locals out of their money.

Preying on people. Ruining more lives than just Jennie's and Patrick's. Martin had learned how to be a man from his father. He'd run off to the army, but even that kind of structure didn't change who a person was at their core.

Was Martin his father's son, or had he done what most people struggled to do and broken the cycle of how he'd been raised?

Eric wandered over. Patrick met him halfway with Tucker so Jennie didn't have to listen to whatever was said. He'd figure out how to tell her later. Though, from the look on her face, he imagined she knew a lot of it.

"I spoke with an MP at the base where Martin Wilson is *supposed* to be."

Patrick stilled. "What?"

"Fourteen months ago, he went AWOL. Came back from a deployment, went on leave. At the end of the two weeks, he never reported in. He'd left his phone—everything— behind on base, only had one bag of clothes. They haven't been able to find him since."

"He's here."

Eric grinned. "It was very satisfying to inform them of that fact. Even though it's not like we were looking for the guy." He folded his arms. "They're sending over a couple of MPs. Boots on the ground."

"Assistance?"

"They're interested in Martin Wilson being put in

cuffs. Evidently he needs to answer some questions about an incident that happened in Afghanistan."

But they weren't going to help with whatever Martin had been up to for the fourteen months since anyone had last seen him.

Eric nodded at the expression on Patrick's face. "Yeah. Pretty much."

He shook his head.

"Don't need their help anyway, right?" Eric said. "Only there's really no way to actually say that without sounding whiny and then making people wonder if you think maybe you *could* use their help."

"We don't need it."

Eric nodded. "Exactly."

"Did you figure out accommodations?"

"You really should check your email. I got you a local short-term rental I booked under an alias I used for the last undercover job."

That had been over toward Arizona, and everyone involved was in jail now. There wouldn't be any blowback or a risk of anyone showing up for revenge.

Patrick let out a huge exhale. "Thanks."

"All the information is in your in-box. Address, door code. Everything."

"And you?"

"I've been thinking about that." Eric scratched at his chin. "If her brother was here, and he's trying to make contact with Nate for whatever reason…" Before Patrick could argue with him, Eric continued, "Means he could be watching."

"Waiting for us to leave, so he can make an approach," Patrick said. "What are you thinking?"

"It involves you giving me your car keys."

"You think pretending to be me will fly?" Patrick grinned.

At least Eric hadn't offered to take Tucker, to complete the ruse. Eric and Tucker had a somewhat antagonistic relationship. They were like two kids, or siblings, each one intent on annoying the other until one or the other had the upper hand.

Patrick said, "You want to pretend to be me, and draw him out. It'll only work if there's someone on the other end to catch him."

"Or it'll be enough to draw him away, give you guys time to get to the house."

"A distraction."

Eric shrugged one shoulder.

His partner was willing to put himself in harm's way so Patrick could get Jennie and Nate to a safe place?

"I looked into the father."

Patrick said, "Yeah?"

Eric nodded. "He used the land, and neighboring lands he…acquired, to transport drugs."

"Including the land he got from my mother."

"Never legally. It's not like Jennie inherited everything he had and is now some kind of land mogul. She doesn't own your old house. She got the house she grew up in and the land around it. That's all in her name now, because it was left to her by her mother."

"So her father strong-armed the town into getting what he wanted, but never on paper. You think the sheriff was in his pocket?"

"If he was," Eric said, "Martin could be up to the same thing. Took over Dad's business after he died. Kept it running through a middle man. When things got heated in the army, he split and came home to run it in person."

"Sounds like some mob boss still giving orders from prison."

"Only he was in the military."

"It's a pretty good cover," Patrick said. "No one would think he was behind it, given he's either across the country or deployed."

Even Jennie hadn't given her brother a second thought. Until he was brought up.

"The MP I spoke to told me they tried to contact Jennie to find out if she'd seen him, but she totally ghosted them," Eric said. "Never returned any calls. He said they spoke with the sheriff, who told them to leave her alone. That she was done with her family."

Patrick felt his eyebrows rise for about the hundredth time. Yet more surprises. "Maybe I was wrong to doubt him."

"Are you going to trust him with this now?"

Patrick shook his head. "No way."

"Okay, good. I was worried for a second."

"If I thought we needed a task force, I'd make a call. But Jennie was right to contact the DEA. They'll want the case if a Wilson is operating in this county again, transporting drugs."

Eric nodded. "We keep her and Nate safe. The army picks up Martin, and the DEA can mop up the rest of them. The sheriff will probably take credit for the whole thing, when we all know who the real hero is." He tried to pet Tucker, but the dog only sniffed at his hand.

"As long as Jennie and Nate are safe."

Eric glanced in their direction. "Mmm. I can see why you might feel that way."

Patrick nudged his partner's shoulder. "Focus. You already let Martin get away once."

"But they are safe. Right?"

Patrick nodded. "Yeah."

Eric pretended he didn't care about the slight. "Let's figure out how we're going to keep them that way."

Patrick grabbed his phone. "Let me call Johns first. See if he has anything from the house and make sure it's been secured."

He figured the men on dirt bikes had cleared out, but he called anyway. There was no answer. Patrick couldn't go check on what was happening. He and Tucker needed to stay with Jennie and Nate.

"Give me your keys." Eric motioned with his fingers. "I'll do double duty, lead Martin away and check on the sheriff."

Patrick dug his keys out. "Please be careful."

"You just don't want to do the paperwork if something happens to me."

"I'm more worried about Tucker. You give him more treats than I do."

Eric laughed as he walked away. But Patrick couldn't join in. Not when instinct told him even one second of a slipup might end in the worst way.

Right now, distraction could cost someone their life.

TWELVE

Patrick shoved the curtain aside and stepped in. Tucker padded to Nate's side and set his chin on the bed.

"Look who it is." The words died on her lips as she realized Patrick was wearing Eric's jacket, holding a ball cap with the word Police across the front.

All his attention was on Nate.

Jennie said, "He woke up a couple of minutes ago. He's still pretty groggy."

Patrick approached the bed. "Hey, buddy."

"Hi." Nate moved his hand and stroked Tucker's head.

She figured her son didn't know what to call him. Patrick or *Dad*. She squeezed Nate's arm, wanting to tell him that they were all new at this. Still figuring it out. This was going to be a whole lot of trial and error.

She said, "The doctor signed off. They're releasing Nate as soon as the nurse comes back with the paperwork and they get a wheelchair up here."

"I can walk."

"You don't think it might be cool to ride in one?" she asked him. "Because that's the only way you're getting out of here."

Nate made a face, his lips mushed together.

"Yeah, yeah." Jennie grinned. If he was giving her that

expression, then he felt pretty good. The lasting effects of being kidnapped would show themselves, and likely wouldn't be physical. But that was a worry for tomorrow. Right now she was concerned about where they would go.

Before she could ask, Patrick eased down onto the side of the bed. "How are you feeling, Nate?"

"Pretty good." His little boy face crinkled into upset.

"What?" Patrick leaned forward. "Tell me what, buddy."

"I—" He glanced at her. Why the guilty look on his face?

"Whatever it is, it's okay," Jennie said.

"I don't wanna go home." He sounded like the little boy he had been, using phrasing he'd grown out of lately.

Jennie pushed away the rush of…grief. And the sheen of tears. He'd lost the feeling of comfort and safety in his own home. That was definitely a reason to grieve.

Patrick answered before she could reply. "My partner found us a place to go. A short-term rental, where we'll be safe."

"Is Tucker going to be there?"

Hearing his voice, the dog jumped up to set both front paws on the side of the bed. Nate laughed.

Patrick said, "Tucker. Off."

The dog hopped down just as the nurse and an orderly came in. The nurse handed Jennie the discharge papers and the orderly helped Nate into the wheelchair. Her son seemed more tired than anything else. Jennie's injuries stung, but she didn't care about that when Nate had a bigger knot on the back of his head than she did. *No concussion.* She had to remember that.

Thank You, God. Keep us safe. Please.

Jennie accepted the paperwork, stuffing the pages in her purse without even reading them. Patrick took the bag she'd packed for herself and Nate and slung it over his shoulder even though he had Tucker's leash, as well.

She walked by Nate's shoulder as they made their way out. "Are you going to tell me what the plan is?"

Patrick glanced over. She wondered if he was even going to answer her whispered question.

"Or why you're wearing Eric's jacket."

"I drew the line at swapping pants," he said. "Especially since he's four inches shorter than me."

She grinned. "And that?" She motioned to the ball cap.

"Oh." He looked down at the hat in his hand. "I almost forgot." He shifted the duffel on his shoulder, and they were off again. The hospital orderly wheeled them in the direction of the elevator.

"Nate."

Her son turned, the hope in his eyes almost too much for her to handle. At just his father's mention of his name.

"Do you wanna wear this?" Patrick asked.

She didn't know if he was aware he'd used the same words as Nate. Stress, fear and anxiety changed how a person spoke and behaved. She wanted her son to meet his father under normal, calm and carefree circumstances. But this was what God had given them.

"It's for me?"

"Yeah, buddy." He settled the ball cap on Nate's head. "Cool!"

Jennie chuckled then covered her mouth with her hand. It was probably a disguise. A way to claim his son and keep Nate's identity under wraps as they left the hospital and headed for what amounted to a safe house.

"Mom! Look at it!"

"It's very cool."

Patrick glanced at her, an expression on his face she hadn't seen in a long time. Behind Nate and the orderly, she reached over and took his free hand. She gave it a squeeze, then loosened her grip. Patrick didn't.

He kept hold of her hand all the way to the elevator, and only let go to push the button so they could go down.

"So you and Eric traded jackets?"

"And he took my car."

She knew there was more he wasn't saying. Patrick wanted to keep them protected, so he was having his partner drive his car. If someone wanted to get to them, they would follow "Patrick."

Or the person might stick around, thinking he'd gone. They would look for Jennie and Nate, who were the real targets.

There was a lot about police work she would never understand. But Patrick had managed to find her and Nate on the worst night of their lives. Now Nate looked at him like his father could do anything. Certain that Patrick could make a plan to keep them safe. The expression looked a whole lot like hero worship.

Jennie would know, because she felt the same way. She always had. And it was clear now that maybe she always would.

That was the deep-down truth. But the wall between that and what she allowed herself to feel was the pain she'd endured for years, thinking he'd abandoned her.

Despite the fact it had been her father's doing, she just couldn't get past the pain. The loneliness she had suffered, raising her son by herself.

Right now was about him getting to know Nate— alongside protecting him. He loved Nate and would be part of his life—and hers because of it. But he'd moved on with his life. Jennie didn't know if she would ever be able to move on with hers.

Not with the hurt so fresh.

Complete the survey below and return it today to receive up to 4 FREE BOOKS and FREE GIFTS guaranteed!

FREE BOOKS GIVEAWAY
Reader Survey

1
Do you prefer books which reflect Christian values?

◯ YES   ◯ NO

2
Do you share your favorite books with friends?

◯ YES   ◯ NO

3
Do you often choose to read instead of watching TV?

◯ YES   ◯ NO

YES! Please send me my Free Rewards, consisting of **2 Free Books from each series I select** and **Free Mystery Gifts**. I understand that I am under no obligation to buy anything, as explained on the back of this card.

❑ **Love Inspired® Romance Larger-Print (122/322 IDL GQ54)**
❑ **Love Inspired® Suspense Larger-Print (107/307 IDL GQ54)**
❑ **Try Both (122/322 & 107/307 IDL GQ6G)**

FIRST NAME   LAST NAME

ADDRESS

APT.#   CITY

STATE/PROV.   ZIP/POSTAL CODE

EMAIL ❑   Please check this box if you would like to receive newsletters and promotional emails from Harlequin Enterprises ULC and its affiliates. You can unsubscribe anytime.

LI/LIS-520-JANFBG21

HARLEQUIN READER SERVICE—Here's how it works:

▲ If offer card is missing write to: Harlequin Reader Service, P.O. Box 1341, Buffalo, NY 14240-8531 or visit www.ReaderService.com ▼

BUSINESS REPLY MAIL
FIRST-CLASS MAIL   PERMIT NO. 717   BUFFALO, NY

POSTAGE WILL BE PAID BY ADDRESSEE

HARLEQUIN READER SERVICE
READER SERVICE
PO BOX 1341
BUFFALO NY 14240-8571

NO POSTAGE
NECESSARY
IF MAILED
IN THE
UNITED STATES

Patrick wasn't here for her, and he wasn't sticking around to get into a relationship. When she fell in love again, it would be with someone for whom she would be the priority. The one that someone was wholly devoted to and would never leave.

As much as she might want things to be otherwise, she had to face facts.

That someone wasn't Patrick. It never had been.

The elevator doors slid open and the orderly wheeled Nate inside. Patrick moved alongside the man in his scrubs. They both shifted at the same time, blocking the doorway so she had to wait to enter. Finally it cleared, and Jennie shifted to follow.

Someone grabbed the back of her jacket, tugging her away from the elevator doors. "What—"

Whoever it was shoved her before she could turn, and she stumbled. Nearly fell.

"Jennie!" Patrick's voice rang out. Tucker barked.

She looked back to see Tucker race out between the doors before they slid shut. Gone. She glanced at the man standing behind her.

One of their kidnappers!

Tucker growled.

The orderly blocked his way to the closed doors. Patrick resisted the urge to shove the man aside.

"Mom!"

Patrick turned to Nate, still seeing in his mind the second she'd been dragged back. Pulled away from the elevator.

"What happened? Where is she?"

"I don't know." Patrick wanted answers to those same questions. He moved to the panel of buttons. Emergency stop? Or should they just try to go back up? "We need to—"

The orderly cut him off. "Don't press any of the buttons."

Patrick turned to him, wondering why the man's tone sounded so threatening. "Why wouldn't I—" He knew the answer to his question and didn't need to finish saying it.

Behind Nate's back, the orderly had a gun pointed at him and his son. Not one of them in particular. But the fact he could shoot either—probably faster than it would take Patrick to pull his gun—wasn't good at all.

He didn't know what to say except, "Don't."

Cold rage settled over him, along with a healthy dose of fear. If something happened to Nate, while he stood there…forced to watch.

His son of only hours—all Patrick had ever had with him—would be dead. Because he'd failed. If Jennie was somewhere, safe and alive, Patrick would have to tell her.

She would never forgive him. Not when he'd promised to take care of them both.

His fingers drifted to his own weapon. But what could he do? Start a war that would result in far too many innocent casualties.

The gunman saw it. "Put that on the floor. Slowly. Then kick it toward me."

Patrick shook his head as he studied the man's face. Not one of the kidnappers Jennie had identified. This man wasn't Martin Wilson, Nate's uncle, either. So who was he? Another man on Martin's payroll. Living on the proceeds of those ill-gotten gains, thinking he could do whatever he wanted with no repercussions from the law.

"You think I'm going to disarm myself?"

No cop worth anything would do that, no matter what was at stake. It was the same as the government's principal not to negotiate with terrorists. Patrick was never going to give all the power to a bad guy with a gun.

Not. Gonna. Happen.

The cop he was, and the father, would never do that. Not when possession of his own weapon meant protecting the innocent here—his son.

"Don't think you've got much play here." The gunman smirked. "So unless you want cop brains all over the elevator, you'll do what I say."

He wasn't going to kill Nate. Whether by principal, which meant he had at least some convictions even if it wasn't much, or because he'd been ordered not to kill the boy... Did the why even matter?

Patrick had that one thing working in his favor. And he was going to use that to get Nate to safety, put this man in cuffs and find Jennie. That was the only acceptable outcome here. Even when all hope was lost, there was always a way to find a victory. His cop mentor had taught him that.

They saw ugly every day. It was easy to forget that there was still good in the world. Right now Patrick needed hope *and* a second chance.

Was this guy one of the dirt bikers, here to get revenge for his maimed friend?

He hadn't counted on them when he'd made his plan, determined to get Nate and Jennie safe from whatever her brother had planned.

Now he realized exactly how thoroughly he'd miscalculated, even with Sheriff Johns providing a female deputy to go with Eric and act as Jennie's double.

Now his K-9 partner was with Jennie instead of here to help him search for her.

First he had to disarm this guy and get Nate to safety.

Then Patrick was going to rescue her. Tucker just had to protect her until he got there.

Nate shifted, still sitting in the wheelchair. *"Dad."*

Before the gunman could react, Patrick said, "I'll get you back to him soon, buddy." He had to play this like the kid was just his charge. Not that he was Nate's father—a man with everything to lose if this went wrong.

Or if the gunman recognized precisely how much leverage he had.

Nate sniffed. Patrick wouldn't blame him if he gave away too much. That wouldn't be fair. He was a smart kid, but even a rookie cop could unintentionally divulge information in a high-stress situation.

"I'm not going to let you take the boy." Patrick motioned at Nate with a flick of his fingers. "You think I won't get fired if I let something happen to him?"

The gunman's lips puffed out, his expression belligerent. "You think I care?"

"I'll be better off dead with benefits for my family than alive and disgraced, with nothing. So go ahead." Patrick patted his shirt—underneath which was a vest.

Any second now, the elevator doors would open. He needed a distraction. Anything. Something. The upper hand, even for a split second, to get the jump on this guy.

The gunman studied him, probably trying to figure out if Patrick was just reckless or if he was actually serious.

Anything to buy him a few extra seconds.

"What's the plan, huh? Take him to your boss. For what?"

"What do you care?" the gunman asked. "You'll be dead."

"Answering a question with another question. Typical." Patrick rolled his eyes. It probably didn't look right.

He wasn't sure if he'd actually ever rolled his eyes before in his life. "But I don't think you'll get far. This is a hospital. Cops. Security. They're all here, protecting the woman and her son. You know, considering they were kidnapped and all."

The gunman's lips twitched. "Heard about that. Shame I wasn't in on it."

Patrick didn't like the look in his eyes at all. The only source of comfort was the fact that Tucker was likely protecting Jennie right now. No way would anyone be able to take her again, not with his dog there.

Nate twisted in his chair to look at the man. He reached down for the wheels and turned them opposite directions, rotating the wheelchair toward the gunman.

What was he…?

"You're going to die. The kid and me are leaving."

Patrick pressed his lips together. *At least say it right.* "That's not going to happen."

"Then you'll be dead before the doors open."

He wasn't sure that was true. Patrick wondered if he'd ever killed anyone before, and if he had the stomach to do it now. Still, regardless of the perceived threat level he had to get this situation resolved.

The only thing Patrick could think to do was pray. *I asked Jennie to pray. You were supposed to be protecting them.*

He wasn't sure how he'd feel about a God who didn't come through for His own children.

"You're dead, and the kid comes with me. If I don't call to say I have him, they kill the mom."

The bottom dropped out of Patrick's stomach.

Jennie.

THIRTEEN

Jennie felt the poke of the gun in her side. She gritted her teeth and tried to think past the barking. "Tucker."

"You tell that dog to shut up." His punishing grip squeezed her arm as he dragged her down the hall. The gun barrel glanced off her ribs.

She sucked in a breath through her nose. "Tucker, be quiet."

The dog leaned forward, ears lifted. Teeth bared as he barked again at the man holding her.

A nurse exited a room in front of her. "What is going on out…"

The gunman's breath hissed in Jennie's ear. "Act natural."

A sob worked its way up her throat. She coughed it back down. Jennie covered the action with her hand and waved the woman off.

Nothing to see here. Just a police dog obviously agitated.

"Tucker." She didn't know what to say to him. Would he even listen to her?

"You shut him up, or I will." He yanked on her arm, squeezing the bandage over her elbow. Jennie cried out.

"Hey!" the nurse yelled.

Three steps from the stairwell—not the spot Jennie wanted him to take her to—the nurse yelled, "Where you guys going?"

The gunman, a man who'd kidnapped her and didn't care one whit if she lived or died, swung around. Cameron? Carl? She didn't remember his name from the police database. All she cared was that his move put Tucker behind him.

The nurse's gaze darted between Jennie and the man who held her in a tight grip. She had a cell phone in her hand. Had she called security?

The nurse put her hand on her hip. "You're just gonna leave without giving me a hug?"

As though behind them both, Tucker wasn't growling to indicate a serious threat.

The nurse was stalling. Jennie said the first thing that came to mind. "You know I'd never do that to you, girl." As though this woman was a longtime girlfriend. Someone she cared about the way she cared about Beth. This nurse was going up against an armed man. She'd read the situation and she was putting her life on the line to intervene.

"We should find that handsome officer so he can come get his dog," the nurse said.

Yes, we should.

"You gonna let her go so she can say bye to me, and I can call that cop?"

Wow, Jennie thought, this woman might be the bravest person she'd ever met. She could've broken down and cried right then and there.

"No." The gunman tugged her backward, to the door for the stairs.

Tucker barked.

"You back off, dog."

No, don't do that, Tucker. But how did she get him to intervene in a way that didn't lead to this horrible man trying to hurt him?

"I'm not going with you." She whispered the words, her gaze wholly on the woman. Pleading with her, and letting the gunman know she wouldn't cooperate.

Praying with all her might that the nurse would understand what was going on.

That she had, in fact, already called security and was just delaying this man. Waiting for them to show up.

Jennie lifted her chin. "Tucker won't let that happen."

"So I fire this gun. Kill you. What happens to your boy then?"

"I'm not letting Martin have him." With her eyes she pleaded with Tucker to…what? He flashed those intense dog teeth and growled.

The man chuckled. His only response to her comment regarding her brother, or his opinion of the animal. It seemed like there was something he knew—or thought he did—that she didn't know yet. Or he was determined to be smug.

Either way, she had to get out of this. Fast. Preferably with no one being hurt in the process.

"On second thought," Jennie said, "take me to my brother. I want to see him."

"Good choice."

She'd find a way to break free of his hold and grab Tucker's leash instead, or this guy would haul her all the way to wherever Martin was hiding. After she spit in her brother's face for what he'd done to her family, she would figure out how to get away.

Everything she'd learned years ago in that very basic self-defense class escaped her now. She could remember a stretch or two—that she couldn't do—from the six months Nate had decided he wanted to be a ninja and she'd taken him to martial arts classes at the local gym.

Then he'd decided he loved animals more and wanted to be a vet.

She was a million percent sure right now that he was going to decide unequivocally that he wanted to be a cop. Probably a K-9 handler. She wouldn't blame him at all. If she was honest with herself, Patrick made her want to be one, too. He and Tucker were both heroes.

"Sir." The nurse looked stern now. "You need to let this woman go."

They were almost at the door. Tucker barked again, his back to the door. Determined not to let them get through. *Good dog.*

Jennie wanted to shake her head, vehemently, at the nurse but she didn't want Tucker to get hurt. Then Jennie would likely be pushed down a flight of stairs. Just because he wasn't there to kill her, didn't mean he needed her hale and hearty when she got wherever they were going.

Behind the nurse, a security guard armed with a stun gun stepped into the hall.

Her heart sank.

Jennie lifted her hands. *Do it. For Nate.* "Everyone just calm down."

"That's right." The gunman dragged her back another step. "Move, dog. We're leaving. Anyone who stops us is going to die!"

"You don't have to do that. Let's just go." She didn't want this to cost anyone their life.

Unless that was what he wanted? Maybe this scene had been inevitable. He hadn't had any plans to go downstairs and this was all just to cause a distraction.

So that someone else could take Nate.

But her son was with Patrick. Nothing would happen to him, not with a cop in the elevator. She wanted to squeeze her eyes shut, take a second and pray, but there was no time. "Please." She could only muster that one word.

And then he tugged her back again. Tucker barked.

The man lifted the gun, so it was pointed past her. At the nurse.

Self-defense. Jennie bent her knees a fraction. In one move, she grabbed his wrist, twisted her hips and swung his whole body around. He basically fell over her. But he was so heavy, she collapsed to her knees and he rolled, arm around her now.

His arm tightened so she couldn't inhale.

Jennie tried to get away from him. The gun went off and someone cried out.

"No!" Jennie had no idea what had even happened.

The gunman waved his weapon around. Tucker closed in, barking loudly enough to make her wince.

"Shoot him!" That sounded like the nurse.

A man said, "I'll hit her!"

Jennie tried to scramble to her feet and get out of the line of fire. She couldn't think. The gun slammed into her temple and her vision sparked with stars.

She wasn't going with this man. She was going to fight the way Tucker was, for her life and for the life of her son. His father. Her family.

Jennie jabbed back with her elbow and hit something solid. The gunman grunted. A heavy weight slammed into her. Maybe the gunman, too. Warm fur. *Tucker.*

Jennie hit the floor and everything went black.

Patrick was so focused on protecting his son from the man with the gun, he didn't see how it began. He heard a grunt and before he realized what Nate was up to, his son had moved.

Nate gripped the wheel bars, turned the chair with a twist and flung out one leg. The gunman groaned and fell back against the wall, but he didn't go down. Nate didn't have enough momentum or strength to do any damage. But it was sufficient to distract their assailant.

Behind the gunman, the elevator doors slid open. Patrick dived. He slammed into him and took the guy to the ground.

They hit the floor in a tumble. The man grunted again. Patrick grabbed his wrist and wrestled for control of the gun. He didn't exactly play fair, elbowing the man in the stomach so he struggled for a breath, but the life of his son was at stake.

The gunman roared.

Tucker barked.

"Tucker!" That was Nate.

Patrick slammed the gunman's wrist on the floor and the weapon skittered away. He lifted up and off the guy, then turned him onto his front and secured him with cuffs. He then patted him down; no phone, no wallet. Not even a gum wrapper.

"Nate?" He glanced back and saw the empty wheelchair. Where was…? Nate peered around the corner, still in the elevator but out of the way of flying bullets. "You okay?"

The boy stepped out, looking nervous.

"He's cuffed. He won't hurt you."

"I heard Tucker."

A second later, Patrick's dog rounded the corner, his leash dragging along the floor behind him, and raced over. Patrick retrieved the discarded gun and tucked it in the back of his waistband. Then he motioned for Nate to come to him. Tucker got there first, skidding on the tiled floor when his paws lost traction and slamming into Patrick's leg. "Hey, Tuck. Did you do a good job?"

Nate giggled. Patrick figured he was less likely to go into shock if he kept moving. Processing. When a person froze up, problems occurred. So he picked up the leash and said, "Let's walk."

Nate eyed the man lying prone on the floor.

A security guard approached. "State police?"

Patrick nodded. "Officer Sanders."

"We've got another one of these guys upstairs. Secured him and called in the sheriff. He's sending someone over to pick him up."

He wanted to ask about Jennie. "They should take this guy, as well."

"This your case?"

"Johns needs to question them, since they're locals and so were the victims. I'm going to stick around and work protection."

"Mom!"

Patrick turned and saw her approaching across the lobby, walking with a nurse.

Nate collided with her halfway, wrapped his arms around her middle, and they hugged. Tucker strained at the leash to go, too. Patrick had to make sure the gunman wasn't going to try anything. But before he turned back to the security guard, and the job he was there to do, he met Jennie's gaze. He mouthed, *You okay?*

She nodded, relief clear on her face, and called back, "Tucker saved me."

"Can you take charge of this guy?" He motioned from the security guard to the cuffed man. When the guard nodded, Patrick pulled the gunman to his feet and rounded on him. "Who sent you here?"

The man stared ahead, saying nothing.

Tucker growled.

"Does the name Martin Wilson mean anything to you?"

A flicker in the skin around his eyes indicated... something. But he still said nothing.

"What does he want with his sister and nephew?"

Patrick didn't much care about motive, but if Martin had something planned then Patrick needed to know what that was. Knowledge being power, it also meant it'd be easier to take care of Jennie and Nate. To keep them safe for good.

Clearly, there was something Martin wanted but didn't yet have. And it seemed that he was still trying to get it.

"Fine." Patrick took a step back. "I guess you can tell the sheriff instead."

"Sure," the guy finally said. "After he calls my lawyer."

A sheriff's deputy strode in, and Patrick explained everything. After the deputy had the security guard—whom he apparently knew—confirm it all, he took the gunman and the weapon.

Patrick turned to where Jennie now sat, Nate close to her side. Both sipped from paper cups, and a doctor was crouched in front of Jennie. She shook her head then caught Patrick's stare.

He took two steps toward them and his phone rang. It was Eric. He answered, lifting one finger for her to hang on while Tucker kept going. She gave him a short nod.

"Sanders." He clicked his tongue for his dog to wait.

"No one followed us. We drove around town a few times, I dropped off the deputy and she followed while I circled again," Eric said. "You guys good?"

"It was probably quiet for you because all the focus was on the hospital."

"I'd like to know how it didn't work. I make a pretty convincing Patrick Sanders, thank you very much."

"Sure you do." He smiled to himself. "I don't want to contemplate it, but I think the uncle wants Nate." Even as Patrick spoke the words, the knowledge settled in his stomach like old fried rice. His son was the target.

"You and that dog of yours get them to the house."

"While you work with the sheriff on interrogating the two men he now has in custody."

"Sounds good."

Effectively they'd given each other orders, but it was how their partnership worked. Mutual cooperation and mutual respect. They were equals. Except for Tucker, who had one master and did not think his relationship with Eric required cooperation.

Another smile.

It occurred to Patrick then that he was happy here. Something he'd never have believed would happen in his hometown. Had someone told him that a visit home would involve danger, so many feelings he'd never anticipated and more joy than he'd thought possible, he'd have thought they were crazy.

And yet, this was exactly where life had brought him.

That made him wonder if Jennie might be right to believe in God.

Had He given Patrick all this, when he'd never even asked for anything?

"Later." Eric hung up.

Patrick stowed his phone, ready to get Jennie and Nate to safety. Unless she needed to be admitted to the hospital, he could do that as soon as possible. She tossed the cup in the trash, took Nate's hand and they met him halfway.

Patrick bent his knees to meet his son's gaze. "You okay?"

"Uh-huh." Despite his words, Nate moved closer to Jennie's side. Tucker shifted in as well and sniffed the boy's face until he giggled.

"Worried about all this?"

The boy worked his mouth. Almost like he was chewing on what to answer. He shrugged one shoulder.

"How about you keep me safe, like with that wheelchair move in the elevator, and I'll keep you safe?"

"What wheelchair—" Jennie started to ask.

Nate cut her off, standing a little taller. "Okay."

Patrick nodded. "Okay."

He needed to get the kid a police badge of his own, so he could feel official. Then he'd have the conversation with him about being brave versus being smart.

He glanced from Nate to Jennie. "Ready to go?"

Jennie nodded. "I'm good."

Nate wound one arm around Patrick's waist. That he was still holding on to his mom while he hugged Patrick meant she was tugged up against him.

Patrick wrapped his arms around them both.

FOURTEEN

Jennie gasped awake. Panic clouded her vision. She breathed hard, glanced around and then remembered where she was. Safe.

She heard the jingle of tags and sat up in the bed. Nate lay beside her on the comforter, under a thin blanket instead of as she was—under multiple heavy covers to keep warm. Tucker lay in the hall, just outside the open bedroom door, scratching at the side of his head with his back foot.

Everything was fine. *You're a good dog.* The nurse had told her how Tucker had jumped on the gunman's back, sent both Jennie and her assailant crashing to the floor and enabled the security guard to take down the kidnapper.

My hero.

Jennie lay back and breathed. A moment of calm in the midst of this storm. They were in a safe place. Nate was good. Everything was good.

She repeated the words in her mind.

Everything is good. She mouthed the words then whispered them to the quiet room before she pushed the covers aside and got up.

Not exactly ready to face the world, but hiding never

solved anything. Burying her head in the sand wasn't going to make her brother go away.

Tucker passed her on the way to the door. She reached down and ran her hand along the dog's back as he moved toward the bed, then turned to watch him hop up on the bed and lie down beside her son.

Jennie opened her mouth. Only the thought of Nate waking alone, as panicked as she had, stopped her from calling the dog off the furniture.

Instead, she left them sleeping together and located the hall bathroom. All the while, she tried to figure out what on earth her brother even wanted from her.

Why come after her son? Why take them both, not harming them apart from terrorizing them, and then try again in the hospital? There had to be a reason, but she couldn't see what it was.

Jennie didn't have money. All she had was her mother's land that had been left to her. If they were trespassing, maybe that was what they wanted? Easy access to her back forty. Maybe Martin wanted the house. She had no idea.

It wasn't like she'd been left a fortune—just a paid-for house. Definitely an asset. Especially considering she'd been a young single mom trying to get an online business going that paid utilities and left something over for food and a tiny fun-money budget. Was that what Martin was after?

Jennie wandered through the house, looking around but mostly trying to find Patrick. Surely he hadn't gone far if he intended to protect them.

She found him in the kitchen, stirring something in a big fry pan on the stove, his back to her. Taller. He'd filled out in the last ten years. In a way that she wasn't ashamed to admit—at least to herself—made her mouth water.

Yeah, she was still very attracted to him.

And why not? The boy she'd loved was now a good man. A cop. On the right side of the law, unlike every other man who'd been in her life. He was like a breath of cool desert air. Light in an otherwise dark life.

Since she was admitting things to herself, Jennie decided to quit being in denial. She did want him back in her life. There was a lot of pain associated with his having left her alone and pregnant. Especially since it was the result of a lie. They'd have to work through all that. But she was willing.

Patrick was the perfect missing piece to their family puzzle. Not just the right piece, but the *best* piece. Considering how long they'd lived without him, there was really no time to lose.

Patrick should know how she still felt about him being a part of their family…for good. For real. Forever.

But then, maybe he didn't feel the same way.

She had to fight those age-old inadequacies. They reared their heads whenever there was a risk to be taken, a chance that could turn out wonderfully if she actually measured up. If Jennie threw caution to the wind and went for it. Things that were scary were usually the ones that were worth doing—like raising her son by herself.

But could she take the risk when Nate's heart was on the line here, too? If she and Patrick had only brokenness between them, her son would be able to tell.

Maybe it was better not to say anything at all.

Jennie sucked in a breath, a sniffle. She wasn't crying but Patrick heard it and turned.

His curious expression softened. "Hey. You okay?"

She didn't even know where to start answering that. There was only one thing to say at a time like this. "Is there coffee?"

"Half a pot."

She hunted for a mug in the cupboards. "I'll probably be awake all night, anyway, considering how late I slept. I doubt caffeine will make much difference now."

"Maybe we could…watch a movie later? Just because we're hunkered down waiting for the sheriff to find your brother doesn't mean we can't distract ourselves. And Nate."

She glugged milk into her mug and then sipped. As she drank those few mouthfuls, she used her free hand to put the milk back in the fridge.

When she turned back and lowered the mug, Patrick had a wide smile on his face. "What?"

He shook his head, grinning. "Nothing."

"Hey, coffee is the nectar of life for moms. Probably cops, too, right?"

"That is true. But I can't say I've ever enjoyed it that much." He motioned to her mug with a tip of his spatula.

She eyed the pan. "Is that breakfast or lunch?"

"Well, it's after two. But I'm still planning to call it brunch."

"Sounds good to me. Brunch is yummy."

"I'll endeavor to not disappoint you."

I don't think that's even possible.

"What?"

She blinked. "What?"

He turned back to his pan.

What just happened? She was willing to let him proceed with his tactic of letting it go. There was so much to talk about. Still, this probably wasn't the time for heavy conversation. Maybe she should just keep things light. And let him do the same.

She leaned against the counter. "So, you cook?"

He glanced over his shoulder. "It was that or eat take-out forever. So I had my mom teach me the basics."

Jennie had loved Patrick's mom. She had been warm and loving to Jennie, though never would have replaced Jennie's memories of her own mother. His mom had been accepting, no matter that her father was a criminal no one could bring charges against.

Hopefully that wouldn't hold true with her brother, as well.

What would Patrick's mom think of her now? She didn't want to be all needy about it, but right before they'd left town, things had been…frosty. Now that Jennie knew her father was the one behind their breakup, she understood. Patrick's mom had allowed her opinion of Jennie to be clouded by how she felt about her father.

"What is it?"

Jennie shook her head.

Patrick turned off the stove and closed the distance between them. If he was any nearer, they would be touching. "Tell me what."

"Nothing." She wasn't going to brush him off, though. "Everything."

"I know what you mean." He squeezed her elbows for a second, then dropped his hands, determined not to push anything. If she wanted him closer, she would let him know. "It's been a wild couple of days, where you've had barely any time to think. Let alone work through what has been happening."

Jennie shrugged. "That is true. You're probably used to it."

"Because I'm a cop?" When she nodded, he said, "Most police work isn't nearly as exciting as what you've been through. I've had more than a few tough shifts over the years, so I'm kind of used to it. In a way, at least. Not your normal couple of days, though."

"No. It hasn't been. Our lives are quiet." Tears gathered in her eyes. "This wasn't supposed to happen. I mean… Martin? Really? I've had nothing to do with him since he left, and I like it that way. Why would he come back now? It doesn't make sense that suddenly he shows up, and now he wants to meet Nate?"

He led her to a chair at the table and dished out some of the food he'd made. Just a simple egg scramble. No bacon—which was why Tucker was currently content protecting Nate and not waking the boy up to get in here and locate some smells. And a sample.

Whatever drew the animal to his son, Patrick didn't blame him. He was grateful Tucker had bonded with the boy and was determined to protect him.

One less thing for Patrick to worry about. There were plenty of other things, but with that one, he had yet another reason why maybe he should thank God.

"You're safe." He touched her hand between bites then said, "You're here, and your brother doesn't know where you are."

She nodded.

He decided to just ask her what was occupying his thoughts. "Do you think God protected you?"

"Of course."

"But it's not like everything was fine. I mean, it wasn't exactly terrible, either…" He wasn't sure what he was trying to say. Just that while things hadn't been all right, they also could have been a whole lot worse. Maybe he just wanted her opinion.

She took a sip of her coffee. "I think… I mean I fell down the side of a mountain. I have a couple of scratches and nothing worse. Nate was in the company of serious gunmen. Anything could have happened, especially if we hadn't gotten back to him in time. All he has is a bump on the head. If that wasn't God's work, looking out for us, then I don't know what is."

"I wanted to pray. When you were pulled away, and the elevator doors shut. Maybe God helped Nate swing his chair at the gunman and distract him."

"He and I will be having a talk about that. It was dangerous. He should never have put himself in jeopardy like that."

"I know. I even agree with you. He's a child and it was my job to protect him."

She shook her head. "That's not what I'm talking about."

It wasn't? Patrick figured he should have taken care of the gunman himself. And he had, but not without Nate's assistance. His son was as good as a deputy, or an honorary partner, at this point. He was full of gratitude that the boy had the fortitude to take action like that.

But he should never have been put in the position where he'd needed to do it.

Jennie sighed. "Never mind. It's over, right? You said we're safe here."

Patrick figured they probably needed God's help with that, as well. "You are."

He didn't want her to worry. Plenty of things could potentially go wrong. Part of that involved the answers from Eric, about his interviews with the gunmen they'd arrested, and from the sheriff, due to call back as soon as he and his deputy were done looking around Jennie's land.

She pushed a chunk of potato around her plate, quiet for a moment before she said, "I tried to find you."

Patrick turned to face her. "But we changed our names."

They'd done it so her father wouldn't be able to

threaten them anymore. He'd gotten their land, so he probably would have left them alone anyway. But his mom hadn't wanted to take any chances.

Jennie and Patrick had talked this through already, but at a time when their emotions had been fresh. Now seemed more like the time to give each other the gift of understanding. To give each other grace. The first step toward building something good out of everything that had happened.

"After my father died, I hired that private investigator. I always wondered if he didn't try all that hard. Or if you'd hidden really well." She shrugged one shoulder. "Maybe he took my money and never searched for you at all. Just sent me that canned email about how there was no trace."

They were both at fault. "I'm sorry you were alone. Sorry about what I missed, but also that I didn't get to be here and help you."

"I'm sorry, too."

He squeezed her hand. When he moved to tug his away, she held on tight.

"I was about to go to your house and tell you that I was pregnant, but my father told me you came over already. That you'd been and gone, and I'd missed you."

He nodded. The afternoon they'd beaten the snot out of him because he'd refused a payout her dad would never have given him anyway, and dumped him in the street like trash, he'd limped home to find his mom had already packed the car.

"He said he told you about the baby, and you didn't care." A tear slipped from the corner of her eye. "He even said you asked for money to leave me alone."

"And you really believed him?" The question slipped out before he could decide if it was a bad idea to say it aloud. She had hired that private investigator. Maybe, deep down, she'd known something wasn't right.

"No. Of course not." More tears slipped free. "I went to your house, but you were already gone."

"I sent you letters."

It was her turn to nod. He figured because he'd told her about the letters earlier. Then she said, "I never got them."

"And I never knew you were pregnant." Yes, he was restating what they knew, but it brought with it so much sadness. He just had to get it out. A thought occurred to him. "I wonder if my mom did."

"I think she hated me in the end. Or blamed me for what my father did to the two of you."

"You think if she did know, she'd have purposely not told me?" Patrick wasn't sure. But he did know people in pain did strange and stubborn things sometimes, thinking it was the right choice. "I guess maybe she might've not wanted us to be tied to your family forever. Never able to separate our lives again."

She looked away.

"What's done is done, Jen." But he needed to talk with his mother. "We *are* tied together, and it's a good thing. Nate is amazing. There are a lot of things about what happened that I would want to change, but he isn't one of them. I should have been here. You shouldn't have had to do this alone."

Jennie let go of his hand to wipe her tears away. "Thank you."

"You raised Nate all this time." He leaned close to her and touched her cheeks. "Thank *you*."

Tucker barked. Patrick was out of his chair before it even registered what that particular sound meant. Followed by a series of barks, it usually indicated danger. Tucker needed to alert him to something.

He reached the door to Nate's room and saw the boy, sitting up in bed.

"What is it?" Tucker was at the window to the backyard.

Still barking.

"You're awake." Jennie moved around him and crossed to the bed. "You were probably dreaming."

Nate turned a pale face and shocked expression to Patrick and shook his head. "It wasn't a dream. Someone was out there."

FIFTEEN

Jennie sat beside her son. His face was pale, his chest rising and falling rapidly. Patrick came over, as well. They'd been close just a second ago, and it had been sweet. Now she wanted to glare at him for putting their son in danger. To remind him that he'd promised they would be safe.

But it wasn't Patrick's fault. No, this was down to her brother, which meant it was more Jennie's fault than his. Neither option was all that rational of a conclusion considering her brother was an adult she hadn't seen in years. Martin made his own choices. He was the only one to blame for this.

Patrick stood over the bed. "What did you see, Nate?"

The boy looked up at him. Scared. Did Patrick not know how imposing his tall figure was, standing over the bed like that?

Jennie twisted to face Nate. "Tell us. Okay?" She kept her voice soft and touched his shoulder.

"It wasn't a dream, Mom."

"I know you think—"

"I *know* it wasn't."

Jennie pressed her lips together. Patrick touched her shoulder. He said, "Please tell me what you saw, Nate."

"A man." Nate swallowed. "In a blue jacket."

"Hair color?"

"Brown."

Jennie bit her tongue and kept quiet while Patrick basically interrogated Nate. Was it a dream, or had it actually been real?

"Outside the door," Nate said.

She looked over at the French doors that led out to the backyard. Tucker stood, his focus on the door, his body straight and tight. As though the second Patrick opened it, he would bolt.

"I'm going to take Tucker and look around outside, okay?"

The dog understood enough of what he heard that he bounded over, tail wagging. Animated now, excited to get to work. Patrick got a leash, hooked it on Tucker's collar and led him outside with a command to "Look."

Was there really someone out there? Jennie knew what her son believed, but she didn't want to agree even though there was a high chance he'd actually seen someone. There was no way her brother had found them this quickly, right?

She looked at her son, who stared at the door where his father had gone. She forced her face into a wry expression. "Did you really tackle an armed man in an elevator with a wheelchair?"

Patrick had mentioned a wheelchair move, but she'd had to put the pieces together herself. She didn't know whether to be proud of the man she was raising or horrified.

He blinked. Distraction accomplished. "Saul taught me how to do it."

"Ah." Nate's school friend had a condition that left him wheelchair-bound. He also played in a kids' wheelchair basketball league. "He taught you how to face down gunmen?"

"There was only one. Dad needed my help."

She wanted to groan but forced it back. "That was very brave." And foolish. And he should never have done it. But she knew now that Patrick blamed himself.

"I couldn't hurt him. But I turned like Saul does and kicked him." He frowned. "It didn't really work."

She found the wherewithal to smile. "I'm sure your dad appreciated your help."

He gave a small shrug with one shoulder. "I think he was mad."

"Sometimes adults look and sound like they're mad, but they're actually scared. It can be confusing. You know what I could use?"

He eyed her. "What?"

"Hot chocolate for breakfast."

He grinned, all trace of that earlier fear gone now. "Do you think we have marshmallows?"

"We can certainly look." She figured he needed to use the bathroom, so she said, "Meet me in the kitchen?"

They went their separate ways, but her mother's senses tracked his movements. Like when he locked the bathroom door. When the toilet flushed. She watched out the window, but couldn't see Patrick or Tucker.

Jennie didn't want to be too far from her son, so she met him in the hall and they moved together to the kitchen. She'd have liked to hold his hand, but he hadn't appreciated her doing that for a few years now.

She set the kettle going, and found enough of what she needed to make this work before Patrick came back in.

There was someone out here.

Tucker strained on the leash, his nose scenting the air

as they jogged across the yard. At the far end was a path and a tiny gate they could both hurdle if they had to. But Tucker didn't go near it.

He only moved through the yard, looking for a scent. Over the berm that had been covered with decorative boulders, shrubs and desert bushes.

"Tuck."

The dog halted and Patrick crouched by what had snagged his attention on the ground. A footprint. Just one thick-treaded print, by itself, angled toward the side of the house.

They walked that direction, all the way around to the front door.

Nothing.

When it was clear he wasn't going to find the intruder, Patrick commanded Tucker to heel and they went back to sniff at the gate. Just in case. But there was nothing out there to track.

He'd seen a figure on the far side of the berm when he first stepped out, but there was no one around now. And if Tucker couldn't find a scent, then Patrick would only be walking around and looking randomly. Taking him farther and farther from the house where Jennie and Nate now had no protection.

Once inside, he took Tucker's leash off and fired off a quick text to his mom before he found them in the kitchen. Before Nate turned around, Patrick gave Jennie a small shake of his head.

Still, simply because he hadn't found anyone didn't mean there was no danger.

Tucker moved to Nate, who leaned against the counter by the silverware drawer. The dog turned and sat with his back to the boy, resting against his leg the way Nate rested against the counter.

Patrick said, "That means he trusts you."

Nate petted the dog's head, a frown on his face.

"He's turned so you're behind him. It means he trusts you won't try to hurt him while his back is to you. Like watching his back. The way he's watching your back."

"Did you find the man?" Nate asked.

"No, buddy. I didn't." Patrick quickly added, "But that doesn't mean it was a dream. Just that whoever was there ran off before we could catch him."

Nate was silent.

"You okay?"

Nate shrugged.

"Do you…want a hug?" Patrick shrugged as well, wondering why he felt so nervous.

Across the kitchen, Jennie poured hot water into three mugs, but he knew she was listening. Patrick hugged his son. Their son. She glanced over and shared a smile with him. They'd covered a lot of ground—especially with their earlier conversation. Things were in no way settled, but it definitely felt like they were getting somewhere. He'd thanked her for raising their son. Of all people, Patrick knew what it was like to be raised by a single mother. That also meant he understood how hard it would have been for her over the years.

"Hot chocolate?" She turned, holding the three mugs.

Nate slid onto a stool. "Mom makes the *best* hot chocolate."

Jennie smiled as she slid his mug over then pushed one toward Patrick. His fingers glided over hers. Warmth. Those tingles he remembered from high school.

They might be adults now, but the rush of attraction was still there.

"Are you going to drink yours, Mom?"

Jennie jerked out of her musings, her cheeks flamed.

Before anyone could comment, Patrick's phone rang. When he pulled it out, he saw it was his mom, replying to his text with a call. "Hey, Mom."

Across the breakfast bar, Jennie stiffened.

"Patrick. I thought you were out of town, working."

"I am. I just had a question, though." Was there even an easy way to ask this? He should probably just rip off the bandage. "I'm in Erwin."

She was slow to respond. "What…would you be doing there?"

"There was a missing boy and his mother." Patrick reached over and rubbed Nate's back, between his shoulder blades. "It was Jennie."

"Jennie." His mom breathed her name. Patrick wasn't sure what to make of it.

Jennie took her mug to the sink, where she stared out the window.

Given Nate might have seen someone outside who could still be there despite Tucker's search, Patrick got up and moved to her. He motioned for her to come away from the window. She sniffed and wiped her cheeks before sitting beside Nate.

Patrick took up her spot. "Jennie has a son." Before his mother could ask, he said, "I have a son. His name is Nate."

Jennie reached out and took Nate's hand in hers.

"And he's missing?"

"No, Tucker found him." Patrick and his son shared a smile. "He's safe, and so is Jennie." *Maybe.* His brain insisted on reminding him their safety was currently tenuous at best. He needed Eric to call back, or the sheriff. In the meantime, he was on point protecting them. And while there was definitely nowhere he'd rather be, it would also help if he could investigate this and find her brother.

Talk to the two they had in custody from the hospital. Look for the other man who had taken them.

"Just...wow." His mom exhaled, the rush of breath audible against the phone's microphone.

"I know. It's a lot to take in. I'm having trouble believing it myself, even though he's sitting right in front of me."

"He's there?"

"He looks like me."

Nate's eyes filled with a kind of wonder Patrick didn't even know how to feel. But he was getting there. And it was probably written all over his own face, as well.

"Let me show you. Turn on your video chat." Patrick tapped the screen to change their phone call to a video call. Then she'd be able to see her grandson. He moved around the breakfast bar and pointed the camera at the two of them while he stood behind Nate, his arm over Nate's shoulder.

"I can hold it." Nate took the phone.

The camera image loaded and his mom's face came into view. "Patrick?"

"We can hear you."

Nate smiled wide. "Hi."

His mom gasped. "Hello."

"I'm Nate."

"Hi, Nate," she said. "I guess... I'm your grandma."

Nate chuckled. Patrick hugged his waist. His son said, "Hi, Grandma." It was tentative, but the most beautiful thing he'd ever heard in his life. Except for Jennie, years ago, telling him that she loved him. Two wondrous things he'd been given.

It felt like his heart was going to burst.

His mom started to cry. "Grandma." She smiled wide and dabbed at her face. Just like Jennie had done.

He glanced at Jennie, but she didn't look at him. Two women he respected. Loved, even. In a way, he always would love Jennie. That was something he'd known since they'd driven out of town. She had been everything he'd needed and wanted in high school.

It astounded him that he now had a second chance. It made him want to believe there really was a God, and He had actually blessed Patrick with everything he needed to fill all those empty, lonely places inside.

"How can this be?"

Patrick moved to the side so he could ask her a question where it was a bit more private. "When we left Erwin, did you know that Jennie was pregnant?"

His mom blustered. "Of course not. Her father nearly killed you. And now you have a son? Just another way to bring you around to her way of thinking."

Jennie let out a whimpering sound. She raced from the stool, down the hall to the bedroom. A second later, the door slammed.

"That was mean." Nate hopped off the stool and stood.

"She didn't mean it," Patrick said. "She doesn't know what's been happening here." And as soon as he could explain it all to his mother, along with what had happened for Jennie since she'd learned she was pregnant, surely his mother would soften toward her.

His mom said, "How could you not have known, Patrick? How could she not have told you?"

He and Nate stared at each other. Torn between their mothers. He was tempted to pray that split wouldn't result in tearing them apart. "I'm going in the other room. Will you get Tucker's toy?"

Nate nodded.

His mom, thankfully, remained silent. Patrick needed to wade carefully through this.

Nothing was going to shake what they were building.

In the bonus room the owners had fixed up like a rec room, Patrick turned the video call back to a regular phone call and put the cell to his ear. "You need to listen to me, Mom."

Nate came in with Tucker's tug toy, and the two started to play. Thankfully out of earshot. Patrick said, "You have to understand that Jennie thought I knew she was pregnant. Her dad told her I asked for money to go away."

She gasped. "You would never have accepted that money, and he would never have given it to you."

"I know that. She faltered in her belief in me and I have to figure out how to forgive her for it. We were gone, and she never got my letters."

His mom fell silent.

"I have a son, Mom."

Nate glanced over from nudging balls across the pool table while Tucker sniffed the carpet underneath. His son and the dog who'd adopted him. There was no going back now.

"I can't believe this." The anger had dissipated. She sounded sad now.

"You need to see Nate in person. Then you'll realize what a great job Jennie did. He's amazing."

The boy blushed, his attention elsewhere, but clearly listening to every word of the conversation. Maybe Patrick didn't have as much work to do as he'd thought. His mom did, though. Nate wasn't the kind of kid who would accept a grandma at odds with the mother he adored, the one who had saved his life.

A scream rang out from the kitchen.

"Mom!"

Patrick hung up and raced after his son. He'd thought she was in the bedroom.

"Tuck!" The dog responded by getting in front of Nate in a protective stance. Patrick ushered both of them into the hall bathroom. "Stay here."

"But—"

Patrick cut him off. "I love you. Please, stay here with Tucker." To the dog he said, "Guard."

No one would get through that door.

Patrick raced down the hall. "Jennie!"

SIXTEEN

She heard him call her name. *Rick.* Jennie turned from the sink.

He raced into the kitchen and practically skidded to a halt.

"Nate." It wasn't a question and yet it was. Where is he? How is he?

"Stop!"

She paused, her foot raised to step toward him. Jennie looked down. Right. She'd dropped a glass in the middle of her freak-out and now there were shattered pieces all over the floor. But was that the point? "Where's Nate?"

He moved to her. "In the bathroom with Tucker. He's safe, and Tucker is guarding him." He stopped and surveyed the room as though attempting to figure out a problem. "What happened?"

"I saw my brother. Outside the window. There were two of them."

She wanted to ask if he was sure Nate was okay, but would that even be helpful? Not likely. Jennie needed to get around the glass and get to him so she could make sure. Not that she doubted Patrick. Of course not. After the last couple days, and what she'd just seen, she needed to reassure herself.

Jennie braced her weight and hopped up to sit on the kitchen counter. She scooted to the end and jumped down. Not the most hygienic of moves, but she didn't want to step on broken glass.

Patrick met her. When she landed, he swept her into his arms.

And didn't let go.

She lifted her chin. "Rick…"

"He's here."

She nodded. That should be the focus right now. The fact her brother was here, along with another man. That meant Patrick was outnumbered. "We should make sure Nate is safe."

"You think Tucker will allow anything to happen to him? At least not without a whole lot of barking to alert me that something is up?"

Jennie relaxed a little, which only served to bring her into closer contact, still tucked against him. Safe in his arms.

He slid his arms from around her and stepped away. A second later, he touched the side of her head and kissed her forehead. "I should call this in. Get backup here."

Jennie flushed. In the heat of the moment she could hardly remember the reasons why falling for him all over again was a bad idea.

Patrick pulled out his phone. She walked to the hall. "Nate? You okay?"

"Yeah, Mom!" His voice sounded shaky, but he was all right. "What's happening?"

"I just dropped a cup, okay?" She didn't want him to worry that his uncle and one of the kidnappers were outside. He would only freak out even more now than he had before. Like she was right now.

"Stay there for another minute. There's broken glass out here and I don't want Tucker to get a cut."

"Okay!"

Giving him a job, and something to focus on—an animal to take care of—would keep him occupied while Patrick figured out what they were going to do.

Jennie got a broom and dustpan from the utility closet to sweep up the glass. She'd been so shocked at seeing her brother trying to hide out of sight. But she'd seen both him and his friend. They were getting ready for something. Preparing to come in, and take Nate from her? She would use this broom, and not for sweeping the floor.

If Martin thought he was going to kidnap her son, he would regret facing her.

The bravado bled away pretty quickly, though. Replaced by the jitters and the shakes. She glanced over at Patrick, jabbing buttons on his phone and muttering to himself.

"What is it?"

"Eric didn't answer." He lifted the phone to his ear. "I'm calling Sheriff Johns."

She'd figured his partner and the sheriff were busy interrogating the men that had been captured at the hospital. But she had also thought that the sheriff was going to her house to check things out. She wasn't a cop, so she'd have no idea what the situation was until Patrick got off the phone and she could ask him.

The same way she planned to ask what the deal was with his mother.

Jennie kept sweeping as she blinked away tears. Hearing his mother's voice over that call had hit her harder than she'd anticipated. She'd been swept up in the tide of it. The love she'd had for his mom, a woman who had meant so much to her back in high school. Jennie had lost her mother at a young age, so she barely remembered her.

Patrick's mom had filled a void, providing support. A sounding board. Maybe she'd told her too much, and his mother had put two and two together when the intimidation started to heat up. She'd figured out it was all Jennie's dad. Then she'd taken her anger and frustration out on Jennie, seeing her as part of the problem instead of what she'd wanted to be.

Part of their family.

Tucker let out a sharp bark.

"No! Tucker!" Her son's cry followed.

Jennie dropped the broom and ran to the hall. The back door, at the end of the hall, was wide open. She raced to it. Before she could run out, Patrick tugged her away. "Stay here."

Because that worked so well?

She followed him outside, but stood on the top concrete step and tried to find…

"Nate!"

Where was he?

Tucker barked again as he faced off with her brother's friend—the second one of her kidnappers. The man kicked out at the dog. Tucker latched on to the kidnapper's pant leg.

Patrick planted his feet wide. "Police! Let me see your hands!"

Jennie searched the whole area for a sign of Nate. Where was he? Still in the house or out here? Maybe he was still in the bathroom.

But when she checked, she didn't see him.

Back at the door, she looked outside again. Nothing. "Nate! Where are you?"

No reply.

"On your knees! Hands behind your head!"

The kidnapper knelt.

She ran over. "Where is my son?!" Her foot caught on a rut in the dirt and she sprawled over.

"Jennie!"

She looked up. "I'm—"

The kidnapper tackled Patrick from behind. A single shove, and Patrick stumbled. Tucker barked and the man raced into the trees.

Instead of following him, Patrick sprinted toward her. She thought he was going to help her to her feet, but he ran inside.

Jennie followed him, but Tucker beat her inside.

When Patrick reappeared, holding a shirt belonging to Nate, she shook her head. Her brother was still out there, and Patrick was messing with a shirt? "You should have gone after that guy. You could have interrogated him until he told you where Nate is and what's going on."

Patrick closed the gap between them and touched his lips hers. "Get your shoes."

What was…?

He held the shirt in front of Tucker's nose. "Scent." The dog stuck his snout in the shirt, nostrils moving. Jennie could hear him taking in air.

She realized what they were doing and ran for some shoes.

The second Tucker moved back from the shirt, Patrick said, "Find."

The familiar pull of Tucker on the end of the leash settled his stomach, at least some. Up ahead was another neighborhood. Streets. People who could be witnesses. This was work. This, they could do. The worry of a parent was unfamiliar, and Patrick didn't know how to begin to control it.

Last time Nate had been missing, Patrick had been a cop and Nate the victim. Now Patrick was both cop and parent, with the victim being his son.

If Eric was there, he'd be taking lead.

If he'd answer his phone.

Patrick gritted his teeth. He glanced back to make sure Jennie was right behind him. She was flushed, probably more with worry than exertion. She wasn't unfit. But she had hit her head recently, and been knocked out. He'd have to make sure she remained all right. Otherwise she would become a liability that would delay him finding Nate.

Then again, Patrick had zero intention of letting her out of his sight.

Okay, God. If You really are there, then I need Your help. Keep us safe. Together. Help us find Nate.

He wondered then what "together" meant. Here with each other…or more than that.

Tucker took a left turn. Patrick should load the GPS on his phone and figure out where they might be headed. He unlocked the device and handed it to Jennie.

"Find a map. Figure out where we might be going, yeah? But be careful. You don't want to trip and twist your ankle."

She nodded.

He faced forward again, trying not to think about that kiss. Heat of the moment. He knew she'd been scared. How else was he going to reassure her? Maybe it was selfish, and it was actually him who'd needed reassuring.

Would he have to apologize later?

"We're almost to the edge of town. After that we're in the middle of nowhere," Jennie said. "But there's a road up ahead."

So Martin could have taken their son along this route

to get him to that road, where presumably he'd had a car waiting. Or he was being shuffled into another house.

Patrick picked up his pace. "Are you good?"

"Yes." That breathy voice had returned. "Let's just get him back."

Nate was the priority. Over everything, including their safety and their emotions. He knew if the rescue wound up costing him a future relationship with Jennie in some way, it didn't matter. As long as they got Nate back.

He wasn't prepared to give up anyone's life except his own. Though he knew what Tucker was prepared to do to protect the ones he cared about. The dog was relentless, and Patrick knew he wouldn't care if he had to give his life for any of them.

Jennie could stay back. Patrick and his K-9 were going to get their boy. There was no other result that was even remotely acceptable.

"How did it even happen?"

He didn't look at her, just kept going. Right to Nate. "I don't know."

Except that he'd been distracted. She'd seen her brother out front, along with a friend of his. Had that been the distraction? Get Patrick away from Nate, leaving the boy exposed. But Nate had been in the bathroom. Which meant either Martin or his friend had to have opened the unlocked back door. Perhaps Nate heard the sound and thought the coast was clear enough to come out. Or at least enough to take the dog out the back.

"We'll find him, right?"

"Yes." He realized how short the word had sounded. But he couldn't explain because his phone rang. She handed it to him. "Sanders."

"Hey." It was Eric.

"Where have you been? Martin came to the house.

Somehow he found out where we were and he took Nate. We're in pursuit." It physically hurt to say the words.

"I'm on my way. I'll do that 'find your phone' thing and track your location."

"Okay." He managed to navigate through to the settings to enable that feature without slowing down too much.

"Backup would be good." So long as Eric could get here in time. There was a serious chance this whole thing would be over before he showed up. "What about the sheriff?"

"He found nothing at Jennie's house. No one on the land, no one in the house. Just a bunch of tire tracks. Someone was there, but they're gone now."

Patrick frowned. "And the guys from the hospital?"

"I just came out of interrogating the second one. That's why I didn't answer. Because I was getting answers."

Patrick heard a tone there, at the end. "But?"

"Yeah." Eric sighed. "Word is, he's more ruthless than the father—who had a serious reputation himself. And the brother is worse."

"I know." Patrick had lived it. Being beaten and then run out of town.

"You said he has Nate?"

"Yep."

"I'll be there, fast as I can."

"Thanks." Patrick ended the call and handed the phone to Jennie, so she could look at the map again.

Out in front of him, Tucker pulled on the leash, still chasing the scent trail Nate had left behind. One that apparently wound through this end of town. And not in circles. They were heading somewhere specific. If they went too far, or if there was an interruption in the scent, they would lose precious seconds finding it again.

God, help us.

Patrick was desperate enough to call on God when he wasn't sure he believed in Him. It might not be faith, but it was a start at least.

"What did he say?"

Patrick scanned the area around them. Tucker took another turn. He told Jennie what Eric had said about her brother.

She said nothing until, "This, up ahead, it's the end of..." Jennie's voice trailed off.

"I see that."

Town just...ended.

The last street, last house. Then nothing but dirt and shrubs. Like the landscape he'd found her in last night, which felt like weeks ago but had only been a day.

Tucker barked.

Across the street, a paneled van had been parked on the dirt shoulder at the side of the road, the door on the side still open. He couldn't make out what was inside. Patrick unclipped Tucker's leash and commanded, "Find!"

Tucker darted across the street toward the van and hopped in.

Jennie made to rush after him, but Patrick slid an arm around her waist. "Wait." He pulled his gun as men emerged from every hiding spot. Behind parked cars. A waist-high brick wall to their right. Someone in the van yelped. Tucker barked and growled.

Patrick spun around. There were at least eight men surrounding them, all armed. He shoved Jennie behind him, but they were everywhere. Martin's hired help? They looked like thugs. Street dealers. Men who'd do anything for the right price.

"Nate!" Jennie's cry rang out.

Patrick looked over at the van and saw a gunman drag Nate out onto the street. The boy stumbled but didn't go down. Tucker hopped out, barked once and sat beside the boy. Patrick gave him a hand signal that meant "Stay."

Patrick glanced around at the men gathered. "Let him go."

"No," a man's voice called out.

Jennie gasped as Martin Wilson came into view.

Her brother lifted his chin. "You'll be putting your gun down now." He grinned without humor. "You're surrounded."

SEVENTEEN

Jennie tore her eyes away from her son and stared down her brother. "Why are you doing this?"

Tears rolled down her face. Intellectually she'd known her brother was behind this, a "head" knowledge she had understood. Now her heart knew. The realization brought with it the deep sting of betrayal. Her brother was the one who had repeatedly put her and her son's lives in danger.

Now there were guns pointed at them. Nate was scared. So much so that she could hardly meet his gaze. What was she supposed to do? The mom bloggers never covered how to emerge unscathed from a crowd of angry armed men.

They were shady looking, with scruffy hair and dark circles under their eyes. Baggy clothes with stains. The kind of people she didn't want to stereotype, but if she was walking through town with Nate she would have crossed to the opposite side to steer clear of them. Along with saying a prayer that they would find help, if that was what they were looking for.

Then she looked at her brother. Exactly the same kind of man. What had happened to him? The army? His time since then? Maybe she was staring now at the person he had been all along.

Her son moaned. The dog shifted, moving closer to Nate so he could lean on the boy's leg.

Jennie wanted to drop to the ground and start bawling. Though it would likely look and sound more like scared whining.

As her brother stalked toward her, Jennie realized she had no idea what they were supposed to do.

Patrick still had his weapon out.

Martin's gaze was on him as he lifted his gun. And pointed it at *her*. "You're gonna put that down now."

A muscle flexed in Patrick's jaw.

She tried to speak, but nothing emerged except a moan.

Patrick shifted his grip. The gun slipped around in his hand, rotating until he held the butt of it. One of Martin's men snatched it from his hand. The man kicked his foot into the back of Patrick's knee. He fell, hissing in pain, but making no other sound.

Jennie moved to put her hand on his back. As he stood, she held his arm. "Why are you doing this?" she asked her brother again.

Martin only sneered.

"What do you want?" She shook her head, struggling to believe him capable of involving family in his business affairs. He had to know how she would feel about him kidnapping them. Seriously. How could he not know?

He didn't answer her.

She said, "Why don't you just leave us alone?"

"No can do, little sis."

"You and I are *not* family. This isn't what family does. And the second you thought I wanted you—" she waved her arm, encompassing all of the men around her real family "—and *this*, you gave up the little piece of me that I *might* have considered giving you." She shook her head, vehement now. Shocked to her core that this was happening to her. After all she'd struggled through. The way they'd grown up. The life she'd had with just her and Nate.

Her brother had walked out of her life a long time ago.

"I have to say, I missed the way you get mad at every single thing I do." Martin tipped his head to the side then zeroed in on her with a hard stare. "No, wait. I don't miss that."

"You have to know the army is looking for you. This is only drawing attention to yourself." She wanted to wave Nate over. To have him run to her so she could hold him. But what if he got shot? She didn't want to do anything that would induce these men to hurt her son. Or to hurt Patrick...again.

"I know how to run my business."

"Using *my* land?"

"That land belongs to both of us," he said. "I have as much right to it as you do."

"That's not true. You are no part of this family. Something that was entirely your choice, which you never even bothered to tell me about. You just left. So even if it wasn't completely legally mine, you'd have no part in the ranch. Because you gave it all up."

"Jennie." Patrick's soft voice penetrated, but only a little.

She shifted to square up against her brother again, but Patrick tugged on her elbow. He pulled her close to his side and said, "What do you want, Martin?"

Her brother chuckled. "I guess you have more you owe me than I thought. Including your thanks. Cause you know what? You're welcome." He clapped his hands together, making her jump. "Back together again, right?"

"That has nothing to do with you."

"No?" He grinned.

Why he disagreed, she had no idea. And didn't want to stand around waiting for him to deign to reveal it to them.

"Just tell us what you want." She lifted her chin.

Martin stared at her. "I'll admit, you were a nuisance. Sticking your nose in. Now things are so much worse. Or better." He eyed Patrick. "Depends on how you think about it."

She took a half step back and Patrick put his arm around her waist. She looked at Nate, so sorry that he couldn't be part of the embrace. Tears rolled down his cheeks, causing a new crop to spring free of her eyes and trail down her cheeks. She wanted to mouth *I'm sorry*. As though she'd had any control over this.

God, help us. We need You so badly right now.

She'd forgotten the very thing she had learned all along, raising Nate. Just the two of them. When they had nothing else, they still had everything they needed to get through.

Because they had their Heavenly Father.

I'm sorry, Lord. I should have remembered that You have us in Your hands.

Peace filled her. The kind she'd never felt before.

Patrick lifted both hands. "What do you want?"

"Let's take a ride." Her brother stepped back. "I'll explain when we get there."

"Let Jennie and Nate go with Tucker. Take me."

She wanted to argue that they shouldn't be separated. But maybe he was right. Patrick was a cop. But she and Nate had been together alone for years, and now they had Patrick back she didn't want to lose him all over again.

Martin shook his head. "They come, too."

"Why?" Patrick's tone was hard.

Was he stalling to wait for his partner? Two men

against eight was better than one, but it didn't scream "winning team."

Martin waved his gun around. Jennie and Patrick both flinched as her brother yelled, "Get in the van! Now!"

Patrick jolted forward. "Easy."

They walked toward the paneled van. Jennie stuck out her hand. The second she was close enough, Nate grabbed it.

"Tucker, heel."

The dog moved to Patrick's side and walked with him, step for step. Body tight. Eyes alert. He knew something was wrong. And he'd found Nate.

They climbed in and sat in the back of the van.

Nate huddled against her side. Patrick's arms around both of them. Tucker lay down beside his leg. Head up. Eyes still alert.

She reached over and petted his head. "You're a good dog. Yes, you are."

Patrick looked up and quickly realized where they were heading. A fact that was confirmed when they pulled onto the drive in front of the house.

His house.

Beside him, Jennie gasped, her gaze out the window. "That's your house."

"Not for a long time," he said.

Not since her father had forced them from the ranch and from town, as well. At twelve acres, it wasn't as big as her land. But it had been home, and he'd loved living there with his mom after his dad had left. Long enough ago, he didn't even remember the man. Something Nate would never be able to say about him.

Patrick made sure the two in the front—the driver and front passenger—weren't paying attention as he slid his phone from his pant pocket. Tucker shifted. Jennie had praised him, making Patrick practically melt. It was exactly what they'd all needed at that moment. They were all scared, not just Nate. The break in tension of her petting Tucker had made Nate almost giggle.

He thumbed through to his texts, making sure he made no sound, and sent a message to Eric.

The blow came from out of nowhere.

Jennie gasped.

Pain rolled through his head, sparking in his vision and raising bile into his throat. He didn't even feel it when the phone was snatched out of his hand. But he heard Nate cry.

Patrick hissed out a breath and tried to control his reaction to the pain while Tucker barked. He moved his hand blindly and found the dog's flank. "Quiet."

The bark, way too loud, made the pain in his head worse.

When he managed to lift his head, he saw the front-seat passenger had his phone in hand. "Looks like our cop here was trying to call for help."

Patrick waited for the man to pull a gun and shoot him right now, in front of his family.

But the shot never came. Instead, the man rolled the window down and threw the phone out.

Patrick shut his eyes for a second. The guy had to have hit him over the head with the butt of his gun. But he hadn't killed him.

That meant he either wasn't allowed to do anything to them that Martin hadn't authorized, or they didn't want Patrick dead.

Maybe it was that they didn't want any of them dead. But that only made his pain-filled brain wonder what they *did* want with him, Tucker, Jennie and Nate.

Their family.

The van jolted to a stop and Patrick gritted his teeth as the door slid open and sunlight spilled in. He loved that blazing New Mexico sun. Always had. Other places had cloud cover almost all the time. Who wanted to live somewhere like that?

Tucker hopped out of the van and did some business. Patrick would have preferred he'd done it on Martin's shoe but, sadly, that wasn't meant to be.

"Tuck."

The dog trotted back over to stand by him as Jennie and Nate climbed out and huddled close.

Martin called out, already walking to Patrick's old front door. "Get them inside."

The house looked so run down. Ten years of weathering and neglect brought with it a pang of sadness. It was never like this before. His mom might have supported them both single-handedly, but she'd always planted shrubs and made sure the lattice fence and garden rocks were freshly painted. Even if that paint was a castoff from a friend of a friend who worked construction.

Patrick had Jennie and Nate go ahead of him so he could watch their backs. The second they reached the front steps, Martin motioned to Patrick. "Not you. You stay out here."

Good. Patrick wanted to talk to him. He'd rather have done it when his head wasn't pounding and he didn't feel that warm, wet trickle running down the side of his face that he was pretty sure was blood. But he'd take what he could get.

God, help me be strong.

He wanted to rely on God. Patrick had nothing else, not even his own strength, to lean on.

"Dad."

"I know, buddy." He moved to give Nate a hug, but Martin shoved him back.

"Both of you get in the house. Now."

Jennie winced.

Patrick wanted to give her another kiss. Anything but think about the one he'd given her earlier. He didn't need to be distracted right now.

"Can Tucker stay with me?" Nate sounded braver than Patrick felt right now. Perhaps he was gaining strength with everything that had happened.

He'd turned to Martin, who said, "No. Now obey your elders and *get*." He waved at the door.

Jennie ushered him toward it. "Come on, Nate."

Tucker whined, his weight steady against Patrick's leg as Patrick said, "Just tell me what you want." The quicker this was over, the quicker he could get Jennie and Nate out of here. To somewhere safe they could recuperate.

He was thinking Maui.

When Martin didn't answer, Patrick said, "You don't care about anything but yourself, do you? You're traumatizing both of them." All of them. "And it doesn't bother you one bit."

"Wrong." Martin sneered. "I care about money."

Patrick pressed his lips together, trying not to let disdain for Martin's choices show on his face.

"I care about interruptions in my business. That's where you come in. Since you were good enough to respond to the sheriff's summons, now you'll help me with my problem."

"You coerced him into bringing me here?"

"Not one bit. I hadn't even thought about using a search and rescue dog when I took Jennie and Nate from their house. That was just to scare her so she'd quit calling the cops and the Feds, and then sign her land over to me. Lo and behold, you show up."

Martin lifted his hands and continued, "Lightbulb." He folded his arms across his chest. "You can find my missing truck. She quits calling the law, gives me her land and leaves town. Everyone goes home happy."

"You want me to find a truck?"

This was the first he was hearing about a missing vehicle. They'd played into Martin's hands. Unknowingly, but it was still the truth. Patrick's presence here had made things so much worse for Jennie and Nate. He hadn't wanted his arrival to have done that, even with all they'd gained from him being there.

The truth was out. They would be a family now.

He could explore what was obviously still between him and Jennie—the deep feelings he'd always had for her. They'd never gone away.

Martin shrugged. "I'm an entrepreneur. We have to think on our feet. Two problems, turns out there's one solution."

"You need me."

"Correct."

Patrick's heart sank. "One single hair on either of their heads is touched, and you get *nothing* from me."

Martin laughed. "That's the spirit. There's nothing like a good bargain."

This man was exactly the same as he'd been in high school, but with added experience—which honestly made Patrick more worried right now. Ruthless. Spiteful. He would absolutely hurt them if he thought it would motivate Patrick to do what he wanted.

"I'm supposed to find a truck?"

Martin nodded.

"A truck with drugs in it."

Another nod.

He was tempted to just string Martin along. Instead, he said, "Tucker can't find a truck. And he's not trained to sniff drugs." Since they also didn't have a scent trail, it wasn't as if there'd be anything for the dog to follow. "What do you expect me to do?"

"I expect you to problem solve." Martin waved to one of his guys. "Get me the thing." The man brought him a bundle of material in a grocery bag. Martin held it out. "Here's his sweater. Find this man, I get my truck and the drugs back."

Patrick said nothing.

"If you don't find my drugs, you're all dead." He leaned forward. "All. Four. Of. You."

EIGHTEEN

The hallway closed in around her. Nate huddled close to her side. Gunmen all around. It was dark in here, the walls bare. The floor nothing but broken floorboards and bits of trash.

"It smells in here, Mom."

"I know." She squeezed his shoulder.

Grief rolled through her for what had become of Patrick's house. His mom had taken such good care of it, making sure it was a pleasant place for him to live. A sanctuary from everything that happened outside.

Jennie had modeled her own home for her son on the same principle. A place Nate could rest. Somewhere he *wanted* to come home to at the end of the day, where the atmosphere was one of peace and rest.

Instead, her father had forced Patrick and his mom from their home. Had her brother been using this house since going AWOL from the army?

The man ahead of them shifted. He shoved a door open. "Get in here, kid."

When Nate didn't move from her side, the man reached for him. Both of them stepped back. She stumbled a little but kept them from falling down. She didn't want to know what nasty thing they would land on.

"Let's go, Nate." She tugged him forward so they could enter the room. Safety. Space. Somewhere they could wait together and not be bothered.

"No," the gunman said. "He goes. You're in there." He pointed at a room across the hall.

"We're staying together."

"Those aren't my orders."

"And you do everything my brother tells you?"

"Pays the bills." The man shot her a toothy grin, his stubbled face displaying his amusement. He enjoyed this. She might even be inclined to believe he particularly enjoyed their fear. What horrible things had he done in his life?

Maybe she didn't want to know.

He waved his gun between them and the room. "Now, he goes in there. Got it?"

"No." Anger surged in her. She wanted to stomp her foot. Put her hands on her hips. It worked with a room full of boys at a sleepover. These were just overgrown boys, right? She planned to treat them as such because she was just fed up. "No. We aren't getting separated. My son will stay with me."

The door behind her was shoved open so hard it bounced off the wall. Martin stormed in. "What's going on?"

"You're not separating us."

Beyond him she could see Patrick, standing outside with Tucker. The look of helplessness and fear on his face was surely a match to what was on hers. Neither of them could get their family out of this alone. He'd tried, and they'd slammed his head.

Now there was blood running down the side of his face.

"You'll do as you're told."

Jennie faced down her brother. "Nate is nine years old. He was already kidnapped and terrorized. You're *not* separating us."

She prayed things weren't going to get worse. That her actions now wouldn't cause additional problems for any of them. But this was nonnegotiable. She held Nate to her side.

Martin huffed out a breath. "This is all your fault. I should separate you, considering all the problems you've caused me."

"Because I wouldn't allow you to trespass on *my* land."

He really thought this was her fault? All she'd done was call the authorities. Had she known at the outset that it was her brother, she would probably do the exact same thing as she had before. After all, a criminal didn't get special treatment just because they were family. Especially not when Martin had been absent from her life longer than Nate had been with her.

Seeing him now did nothing more than break her already shattered heart.

The man he could have been was evident when she put him side by side with Patrick. Goodness and evil. There wasn't a greater contrast in life, was there? The ultimate opposites, they would be forever at odds.

She was sad for who he was now—who he thought he should be. The man her father had made him into. She'd had Patrick, and it just hadn't been the same between her and her father. But he'd groomed Martin to follow in his footsteps. To do exactly this.

Still, the life he lived now... On the run, full of not much besides illegal activity to fill his time. He would have to always look over his shoulder. It was all down to his own choices.

The decisions he'd made.

As much as she wanted to be immune to him, a tear rolled down her face anyway.

Martin ignored it. "I'd have been free to do what I wanted if you'd just *left things alone*. Instead you've caused me so many headaches I have a migraine because of you."

She should have called the army back a year ago. They'd have swooped in and taken him into custody, right? Problem solved.

Martin snickered. "I can see you planning something. Well, you know what? It won't work. So don't waste your energy. Keep your son quiet. Patrick does his job, and you get to go free."

"But you'll continue like nothing is wrong?"

"No. I'll be long gone. One last severance payment for everyone I employ and I go live my life. You'll never see me again."

That was enough to make her smile. He would be gone? "Fine." She had every intention of calling the army and telling them everything as soon as she got to a phone. "Nate and I stay together."

"Get in there."

She looked at Patrick. He gave her a short nod, everything he wanted to say plain on his face. She wanted to mouth the words *I love you*, though she wasn't all the way there. Yet. Those feelings were fast coming back.

Jennie had loved him once. Had that ever really gone away? Giving those words to him now would mean everything to her. Yes, there were qualifiers. She was falling for him again. But complicating it with specifics didn't mean much. In a situation like this, she needed to either go for it or not. Their lives were on the line.

Why not her heart, as well?

He lifted his chin. "It'll be okay."

She nodded back. "Okay."

A pact. They were together. Even if they got separated, they'd stick with each other through this. Come out of it a family. Where it wouldn't be too soon or too complicated. She'd be able to tell him the simple truth of how she felt.

Martin strode outside. His man shoved them into the empty room and slammed the door.

Nate walked around the empty space for a second. He settled against the wall and slid down, knees to his chin. Jennie sat beside him.

"I wish Tucker was in here."

She gathered him to her, holding him in her arms. "Sorry, buddy. I guess he needs to work."

Nate made a *pfft* sound through his lips but said nothing.

"We should pray." She didn't wait for him to agree or disagree. It shouldn't matter whether she "felt like it" or not. The situation was out of control and they needed to hand it over to the One who was in control of everything.

Jennie prayed over them, and over Patrick's work with Tucker, asking God to help them get out of this alive.

Nate said, "Amen."

Jennie shuddered. A vibration of fear she could no longer contain.

Help my son to live.

A gun jabbed into his back. Patrick stumbled away from the house. "Okay. Ease up." He turned to them, hands raised. "You got what you wanted, so just lay off, okay?"

Yeah, he was repeating himself. But it seemed like these guys needed an extra hand understanding. He was supposed to find a truck? Martin knew that didn't have a scent. And a man, from his sweater? Sure, if they could find a place where he'd actually been. If they had no idea where he was, how was Patrick supposed to have Tucker find the scent? It would be like finding a needle in a haystack that could be thirty miles away, for all they knew. And drugs? Tucker hadn't been trained as a drug detection dog, so that wasn't a possibility.

Patrick scrubbed both hands down his face. When he looked, Tucker was leaning forward. Body straight, muscles tense. The hair on the back of his neck stood on end. Any second now he would flash his teeth and growl.

He wanted to let the situation escalate in a way Martin would regret, but that would result in Tucker being hurt. Patrick pulled the long leash from the pocket of his cargo pants and snapped it on. "Heel."

Tucker shifted to his side, but didn't back down. Much.

Martin eyed the dog, then said, "We got a problem?"

"What do you think?"

"I think you're going to find my truck."

Patrick didn't even know where to start with that. "He can't find a vehicle. Or a man who's been in a vehicle. If the windows were rolled up, there's no scent. And he's not trained to find drugs."

"He's a search and rescue dog, right? So search for my truck and rescue my drugs."

Patrick blew out a breath. What did this guy expect him to do? It literally wasn't possible. "Do you have an idea of the location where he is, or somewhere he was, like, when you last saw your friend?"

There were a million other questions rolling around in his head, but that was a pretty good start.

"I'll give you what I have."

That sounded more like a threat than an intention to share information. This man was a dangerous loose cannon. After all, he'd lived under the radar for the better part of a year since he'd walked away from the army and disappeared into civilian life—the criminal underworld.

"And I'll have to figure out how to do the impossible, I guess."

Martin shrugged. "The alternative is I kill you and Jennie, take Nate and raise him as my son."

Patrick surged forward. Tucker did the same, barking at Martin.

Jennie's brother lifted his gun and pointed it at Patrick's face.

That was the only thing that stopped him from tackling the guy. Take his son, when he'd just met the boy? Destroy his life, and Jennie's, and all that could be?

"No." He practically stared down the barrel of the gun. Never a good spot to be in. Even with a K-9 partner by his side, Patrick was in serious danger.

"Mmm. I agree."

So this was about control, then. "Just give me what you have and let me do my job. Then, you *will* let us go. Unless you want the army crawling all over this place and breathing down your neck until they finally catch up with you."

"As if they will. I've gotten away with it so far."

"They know you're here." Patrick shrugged one shoulder. "The call's already been made. Wheels are in motion. In fact, it's probably only a matter of hours before they descend on this place en masse."

Boy did it ever feel good to say that to this guy's smug face.

Until Martin slammed the gun down, aiming for the same spot where he'd already been hit. Patrick turned away from him in time. The butt of the gun slammed into his shoulder instead. He grunted at the impact as pain reverberated through his torso.

He straightened. "Everything you have?"

"Good choice." Martin waved to one of his buddies.

The gunman spread a map of the local area on the hood of the van that had brought them here. The kind of map you'd buy at a grocery store. Only this one had penciled lines. Notations. Asterisks. There was a clearly indicated route that cut through the foothills from what had been Patrick's home, across the desert, through Jennie's land, to the highway east of town.

"This is where he was last seen." Martin pressed a dirt-smeared finger north of Jennie's land.

"That's why you were trespassing?" Or, at least, why there'd been an uptick in activity on her land recently.

"He went missing five days ago."

"And you want your drugs?"

"We all have our retirement plans."

Patrick had a lot to do *before* retirement—like get his family back. All of it. The way it should be. But he got what Martin meant. "What's in that truck is your nest egg? How do you know the driver didn't take off with the drugs and he's in Mexico by now?"

Martin pulled out a phone. "GPS. The tracker in the truck went offline. That's how we lost him. Then he never checked in when he should have. But he couldn't have disabled the tracker himself. He didn't even know about it. Besides, he's dumb as a box of rocks. Actually, that's an insult to rocks."

Patrick faced off with Jennie's brother. "Great. Let's go out there and I'll get Tucker to search for a scent. Assuming that item of clothing you've got is even something he can get a scent from."

He was waiting for a hitch in this plan that would mean Martin had no use for them.

So long as his not needing them anymore didn't mean

he would execute them all and leave them out here. Or stage some kind of elaborate murder-suicide scene to throw off the sheriff.

"Is the sheriff in your pocket?"

Martin shrugged. "I might do that. If he actually cared enough to try to get rid of me, I'd probably offer to pay him money."

That didn't answer Patrick's question. Not really. "So he just leaves you alone?"

Martin said, "I don't care about him. Find my truck."

"Give me that sweater so I can use it for a scent." That was better than trying to get a straight answer out of Jennie's brother.

Martin looked about ready to slam him with the gun again, but Patrick didn't care. What more could Martin do, or threaten to do, that hadn't already been done to him by the men in Jennie's family? Then there was the damage they'd done to Jennie. To Nate. They'd been through enough—too much, in fact.

One of the men retrieved the grocery bag holding the sweater.

"Ready to go, Tucker?" He needed to get the dog excited about work. Focused on Patrick, and not the fact he wanted to be in the house with Nate.

I know how you feel.

Martin's phone buzzed. He pulled it from his pocket and muttered under his breath. "The sheriff is headed here. Everyone load up. Now!"

"What about Jennie and Nate?" He wasn't going to give them back to the sheriff, was he? That would mean he'd lost all his leverage.

"They come, too." He turned to his gunman friend. "Get them. Two minutes. Let's move!"

Patrick was shoved toward a car as Jennie and Nate came out.

"What's happening?"

He got close enough to grasp her hand. "The sheriff is coming."

But the happiness on her face was short lived.

One of the gunmen grabbed Nate around the waist and hauled him away from them.

"Mom!"

NINETEEN

"Nate!"

She'd been shoved into that room. Then, only minutes later, she'd been dragged back out. Now Jennie didn't even know what was happening.

The sheriff is coming.

Patrick moved with her. But Martin stepped in front of them, blocking the path to their son. Who had been ripped from her arms.

"Move!" She screamed in her brother's face, tears streaming down her cheeks once again. Maybe they hadn't ever stopped. "You can't keep me from my son."

"Get in the van." Martin looked deadly serious, like he was inclined to shoot whenever he decided to.

She halted, though everything inside her wanted to shove him out of the way—gun or no—and race for Nate.

Her son was currently being dragged away. He kicked and screamed against his captor, struggling to break free of the man's grip. A man who looked like he'd go up against a biker without breaking a sweat. Ruthless. Evil, maybe.

Did she believe in her heart that Martin would actually kill her if she ran for Nate? Maybe not. But he would shoot to maim her.

"Let's go. In the van. *Now.*"

Jennie's body jerked with the force of his order. A sob worked its way up her throat, but she didn't let it out. Crying wouldn't help.

Tucker barked. Jennie sniffled and Patrick tugged her toward the van. Didn't he want to go after Nate? Instead, he was hauling her toward the van. Doing what her brother ordered them to do. Why? Johns was on his way, so that meant they should delay as much as possible to ensure they were still there when he showed up.

The sheriff wasn't in on it. She'd wondered before, but if Martin was purposely avoiding him then the man was a threat to Martin's plans. He wasn't in Martin's pocket. If he was, then it wouldn't make sense for them to run.

She turned to glare at Patrick. *Nate.*

"I know." It was like he knew what she was thinking. Probably it was written on her face. *Good.* He said, "Come on."

He wanted to help Martin by cooperating?

Patrick tugged her on, the muscle in his jaw flexing. Tucker hadn't moved when they had, causing them to bump up against him. The dog barked at the man currently holding Nate where Jennie couldn't reach him.

"Tuck. Heel."

Her brother motioned with the gun. "You keep that dog in line. And no commands to bite anyone."

"He isn't a protection dog. He finds people."

"Good." Her brother nudged the gun into *her* back. "Now get moving." Then he told the man holding Nate, "Take a walk."

The man nodded. He already knew what that meant? Jennie watched, her eyes stinging they were so wide, as Nate was taken from her between the house and the dilapidated old garage Patrick's mom had used for storage.

Martin shoved them to the van. "Get in."

She spun around instead. "Don't let that man hurt him. And don't you let him even *touch* my son. That is your nephew. If you have any good inside you at all, you won't leave him in the hands of someone who could hurt him." Or worse. Some wounds healed. Others were never visible to anyone else, and yet the bearer carried the pain for years.

God, please. Not my son.

Martin shoved her back again. The gun glanced off her collarbone and his other hand slammed into her, toppling her over into the van. Backward, so she fell awkwardly.

Patrick sucked in a breath, sounding like he was in pain. Tucker's tags jingled. Jennie pushed off the floor of the van and winced at the ache where she'd landed.

"Let's go!" Her brother's voice rang out.

Patrick climbed in the van, and she heard Tucker move around her. Jennie curled up. After a second, she realized she was crying.

"Okay." Patrick gathered her into his arms. "Come here, Jen."

She sucked in a choppy breath and let the tears flow.

He pulled her close and held her in the strength of his arms, one hand rubbing up and down her back as the van rumbled along.

"Nate." Her voice was barely a whisper, more like a moan. She squeezed her eyes shut and prayed he would be safe. Unharmed. She could no longer pray he wouldn't be traumatized by this. That was a fact they would all now have to live with. It was real, and it was going to be part of Jennie's future as a mom.

Because they *were* going to get past this. She would get Nate back and they'd move on. With Patrick in their lives.

No matter what, she was going to have God to thank for everything if they were all alive. Life went on.

Jennie lifted her forehead from Patrick's neck and pushed off his shoulders as she sat. She wasn't going to fall apart anymore. Not when God would always be there for her.

"Hey." He touched her cheeks, wiping away tears.

Jennie didn't have any words. She touched her forehead to his and shut her eyes.

"It's gonna be okay. I'll find his guy, and his drugs, and all this will be over."

He wanted her to believe that? Maybe she did and maybe she didn't. But she could agree on faith that the assurance would come later. Despite the circumstances. Despite the prognosis.

That was what faith was.

"The sheriff will show up at my house. Eric, too. They'll realize what's happening and track us all down. This many people together won't go unnoticed for long."

She nodded and lifted her head, opening her eyes. "Thank you for being here."

He'd been called to this job because of his position. Not because of her—at least, not that she could surmise. All she wanted to think about was Nate. But Patrick had come. He was the only man she'd ever loved. Her son's father.

She touched his cheeks then pressed her lips to his. "Thank you."

"There's nowhere else I'd rather be."

God, keep our son safe. It was like a mantra, rolling through her head over and over again.

Patrick held her gaze with his. Soft. Determined. "I'm not leaving. No matter what. I'm going to do this for your brother, and we'll get Nate back. That's nonnegotiable. Okay?"

Like him, she could hardly contemplate losing her son. "I'm not leaving."

She lifted her gaze. Why repeat that? Unless he was coming to care for her, as she was for him. Probably she was way past that right now. Falling for him, when she'd been in love with him for more than ten years?

Jennie was going to trust him. "Good."

The van bounced over a rut in the dirt road and her mouth bounced against his. Her cheek slammed into his jaw. He gritted his teeth. "Sorry."

Jennie squeezed her eyes shut. "Let's just pray for Nate."

"Okay." His arms tightened for a second, imbuing her with another dose of comfort as she spoke her prayer aloud until the van pulled to a stop.

Patrick kissed her forehead and she opened her eyes, shifting so the gunmen and her brother didn't see how close they'd gotten. She felt better, but that didn't even touch the fear she held for Nate. Nothing would cure that. Not until her son was back in her arms.

Safe.

She pulled away, but Patrick still felt her weight against him. Shared warmth. The echo of the feelings roiling inside him. Nate, alone with a dangerous gunman. Held captive until Patrick found this truck, its driver and the drugs inside.

The van door slid open. She scooted away from him, but he touched her arm. "Let me get out first."

He wanted to protect her. It was an imperative now. There was nothing else he could do but keep her as safe as possible. *God, help me keep them both safe.* It was coming more naturally now to lift up a prayer. Something to be thankful for, even in the middle of everything that was happening. Faith grew in him, incrementally with each new occurrence.

Except it seemed like things were only getting worse, not better.

Tucker hopped down.

"Heel." Patrick shortened the distance between them and kept the tension on the leash. Now, more than ever, Tucker needed to know that Patrick was the one in charge.

With his free hand, he kept Jennie behind him, hopefully out of the line of fire. She closed in, one hand on his left hip as she peered around his right shoulder. Close enough she could touch her cheek to his arm.

Martin came over.

"This is where the truck was last seen?" Patrick asked.

They weren't too far from the back portion of Jennie's land. Maybe five miles. They were parked in a dirt lot of an abandoned bar, shut down long enough ago that the windows were boarded up and what remained had been smashed by rocks—probably thrown by local kids messing around.

This place? Jennie's father had reigned as king here. Not surprising Martin had gravitated toward it. Seemed like he'd been trying to take over his father's empire. Resurrect the old days. Because he wanted to be as lucrative as his dad or because he simply missed the old man? This might even have been the place Martin had been living in since he'd walked away from the army. Squatting in an abandoned building was no kind of life, no matter how much cash he had from illegal operations. It wasn't like he was putting it in a savings account for wherever he moved next.

Patrick didn't want Martin trying any of his father's

methods for keeping people in line on him, Tucker or
Jennie. Or Nate.

God, help us.

Martin studied him. "So eager to get started?"

"Let's just do this. The quicker I find your stash, the
quicker we're all done with this," Patrick said. "You know
the cops are on your heels. It's only a matter of time before the sheriff's department—and the army—is breathing down the back of your neck."

Martin grinned. He pulled out his phone and made a
call. When the recipient answered, the only thing he said
was "Do it." Then he hung up and looked at the scenery
to the west.

An explosive blast shuddered the sky. The fireball
rolled up into the air from a structure over there, and
wind blew at them in a single gust.

Jennie huddled closer to Patrick's back. "Was that the
garage?"

Nate. His son hadn't been inside. But that didn't mean
Martin lacked the means to make good on his threats.

"Don't worry about the sheriff, or anyone else finding us," Martin said. "I'm not."

Well, he was. Patrick was also worried about Eric. His
partner was smart, but that didn't mean he couldn't ever
be caught unawares.

"Give me the bag. Tucker can get started."

If there was even a scent to find and the truck driver
had been traveling with the windows down to leave a
trail, and recently enough that the scent would still lin-
ger. And yet, given everything Jennie had told him had
been going on, it must have been long enough at least one
weather front had rolled across this desert.

There was probably nothing left to find.

He still figured the most likely thing that had happened was that the man had taken the drugs and made a run for it. He was likely hiding in Mexico, or somewhere he could stay under the radar, and off-loading the merchandise to someone who would pay cash and ask no questions.

Patrick just had to string Martin along long enough for Eric to catch up with them. Or the sheriff, the DEA or the army. Patrick was feeling pretty equal-opportunity about their rescue.

But help would come.

I believe, Lord. Help me do this.

Martin's guy gave him the grocery bag containing the sweater. Patrick bemoaned the fact he'd never trained Tucker to fake finding a scent. Maybe they should try that. Though, it would be seriously difficult to get a scent dog to do the work under a separate set of commands when there was nothing and he had no idea where to go because he wasn't following anything. Go in circles? Go for a run?

That was a problem for another time.

"Scent." He held out the bag.

When Tucker had sniffed the contents enough, Patrick handed back the bag and they set off.

Tucker headed for the building. He circled around, sniffing the wall in a couple of places.

"He isn't in there."

Patrick didn't look back at Martin. "Doesn't matter. This could take a while. That's why I wanted to get started. If your man is miles from here, we could be doing this all day."

"Okay." The tone was like he'd said "So?"

Patrick tried not to glare at the sarcasm. "I just want to know Nate is all right."

He followed Tucker away from the highway and into

the desert. There wasn't a road out here. Had the man he was looking for walked out into the middle of nowhere?

He didn't like the scenarios going through his head.

"Me, too," Jennie said. "I want to know Nate is okay."

One glance at Martin, walking behind them, told Patrick the man didn't much care what Jennie or Patrick intended to do. Patrick said, "You need me. And Tucker. One command and he lays down."

"One command and your son starts bleeding."

Patrick pressed his lips together. "Just let me know he's all right."

It took Martin a minute to make the call. When it was answered he said, "Yeah. Put the kid on."

Patrick glanced back.

Jennie held the phone, now on the line with their son.

"Hi." Relief washed over her face. "You okay?" She listened, her lips pressed into a thin line.

After a minute, Martin snatched the phone back and hung up. "Now you know."

Patrick set off in a slow jog. Tucker had something.

He picked up his pace for another twenty minutes, until they were almost two miles from the building by his guess. That was when Tucker found the man.

Patrick saw him first. Before anyone else could catch up and see, he tugged on the leash. "Heel." When Tucker came to him, Patrick said, "Good boy," and petted his head.

Tucker was confused. He hadn't sat to let his master know he'd completed the task.

Patrick praised Tucker as if he had, while he tried to figure out what to do.

The truck was nowhere in sight.

"What is it?" Martin picked up his pace and approached.

Jennie didn't look like she was doing very well. Her face had flushed, and she was breathing hard. He figured she needed to sit, with Nate on her lap.

"Well?" Martin waved at the desert in front of him.

"He's right there." Patrick indicated the area where Tucker had stopped. A man lay on the ground, facedown. "Is that your guy?"

He knew the answer to that, even before Martin rolled him over. And then kicked the dead man in the leg while he yelled out his frustration. "Where are my drugs?"

TWENTY

Jennie turned away from the dead man. Bile rose, anyway, and she had to pace a few steps farther to an out-of-the-way spot where she could spit. There was nothing in her stomach to deposit on this middle-of-nowhere land, no matter if she wanted to throw up or not.

He was dead. Really dead. Not that there was a midpoint where someone was partially dead. Especially when they'd very obviously been out here a while given the flies.

"You okay?"

She turned to Patrick. His expression was one of sympathy. He didn't think less of her for reacting like this to a dead guy?

Jennie managed to nod. "I'm good." As soon as she could swallow, she would be even better.

There was so much going on, though, the state of her stomach didn't really rate. A dead guy? That was a little higher on the scale. She wandered to Patrick and leaned down to pet Tucker. "Is he really dead?"

He nodded. "Sorry. It looks like he hit his head, or maybe was struck."

"So he might have been murdered? Like someone killed him and stole the truck?"

Martin let go of the dead man, done searching the guy's pockets. And his shoes, for some reason, that were now discarded on the dirt. He strode to her. "This was betrayal, not murder. This man worked for me, and I take his death seriously."

"Great." It came out before she could call it back, sarcasm threading through her tone. She couldn't believe anything about her brother now. Who he was. How he was. All of it churned her insides even more than that dead guy.

She folded her arms over her stomach. "You care about your people's lives, but not the lives of your own family? Isn't that just great."

"Don't comment on things you know nothing about."

She shrugged. "People do it all the time online." Why did he care what she said now? He barely thought about her.

Martin shook his head. "If I don't get my money, who do you think is going to die?" He slapped his chest. "This part of your precious *family*."

"You don't care about my life, so why should I care about yours?"

She shouldn't but did. And when did care have anything to do with a person's worth? That wasn't how feelings worked.

"Why will you die if you don't find it?" She was careful to keep her tone even. He was like a bomb about to explode at any moment if she did or said the wrong thing. "Tell me."

"The men who gave me those drugs expect payment. If I can't get it from sales, it comes out of the collateral. My life."

That sounded like a horrible business model. She wished she'd never asked. Jennie could have lived her whole life never knowing that was how the drug business worked. Then again, given her family history, she probably should have put that together. If she'd spent any time at all actually thinking on it—which she hadn't.

"You were nothing but a memory." She faced him down. "Now you're a nightmare come to life."

She'd tried to get him to realize he was hurting his family. Martin didn't care about their lives, even just the tiniest bit. He was oblivious to what he was doing to the people he should always care about, no matter what. Martin cared about nothing but himself. And money. He had no conscience, not anymore.

The only person who had always cared about Jennie, no matter what? Patrick. He and Nate were the only people she could say the same about for herself. Unconditional love. That was what they'd given each other.

Jennie paced away from her brother. Patrick held out his arm, so she walked into his embrace, eyes shut tight to try to block everything out and just focus. Pray. Believe in faith for her son.

But she could get no clarity.

Jennie gave him a squeeze and pulled away. She walked farther. Away from the dead man and her evil brother. She kicked at the ground and tried to wrestle through what she wanted to say to God. She was at the point it was tempting to start making demands, but it didn't work like that. Her Father in Heaven wasn't going to acquiesce just because she tried to force Him to.

Please.

It was all she could manage.

A spot on the ground caught her attention. Dark colored. Not something she usually saw out in her desert. She didn't have the time or the heart to care, whatever it was. Jennie kept going and stomped on it because that was how much she shouldn't care. Not at all. Until she saw another spot.

This whole thing had ruined her ever wanting to hike, camp or try practically any other outdoor activity again. Though, when she got Nate back—not *if*—she'd be happy to do anything he wanted. It didn't matter how she felt. As long as Patrick came, too, she would be safe.

She glanced back at Patrick, but he was in a hushed conversation with Martin. Strong. He'd been disarmed, but that hadn't taken much away from his presence.

Neither man looked happy, both faced off with the other, but she didn't like the tension in Patrick at all. She wanted him to be relaxed. The man she loved should be safe and secure, no worries. Wasn't that the goal in life? Of course not, because bad things happened anyway.

She blew out a breath, wanting to kick at the ground again. "I want my son back!" She wasn't ashamed to yell the words to whomever was listening. Her brother. All of them. Who cared about Martin and his stupid drugs? "I want my son back *now*!"

One of the nearby gunmen snickered.

Great. He thought she was an emotional woman throwing a tantrum. She was, but it was justified.

Jennie stomped toward him. He backed up two paces. "Whoa. Calm down."

"Jennie!" Her brother snapped the word at her.

She swung around to him and yelled like she would have done when they were kids. "What?"

"We're closer than we've been in weeks. Calm down." He scrubbed at his head.

Jennie moved to him. There was another spot on the ground, between her and the…deceased man. He'd been out here awhile and she—

Don't think about that.

She stared at the ground. "What is *that*?"

Patrick moved closer. "Looks like blood droplets. Probably from the dead guy." He looked at Martin. "If we follow them, there might be a trail. Maybe he crashed the truck and tried to walk for help. Could be it was an accident."

Martin studied the ground.

Jennie walked back to where she'd been. "There are more over here. They go this—"

A shot blasted. She froze, too late to avoid it. Dirt had already kicked up from Martin's shot at the ground faster than she ever could have moved.

"Easy!" Patrick said.

Martin waved the gun. "Jennie, get back here. You wander off too far, you're as dead as that guy. I'll leave you out here for the birds."

He saw her shiver. Patrick wanted to do the same, but held himself steady as they followed the blood trail. Would it lead to the source?

He wanted this done. No more gunmen pointing weapons at him, or Jennie. Not even to shoot the ground by her feet and scare her. Patrick wanted Nate back in his arms. All this over with already. *Please, Lord.* He'd been stubborn for so long, it felt freeing to not have to rely on himself for this.

He could simply trust.

Martin studied the ground, content to let his men watch his back. But how long would that last? He was motivated to get his drugs. To save his life. Patrick had thought—from what he'd said—that this was about a nest egg. In a way, it was. But only in the sense that it would keep him alive when the men who'd supplied him with the drugs demanded payment.

"It doesn't have to be like this, you know."

Martin eyed the ground as they walked. Tucker thought they were out for a stroll. He'd never been interested in blood before and didn't seem to be now. He kept turning his head to look back. Making sure Jennie was okay?

Martin said, "This the part where you offer me witness protection?"

"You think you've got enough on these guys to warrant that?" Patrick wasn't afraid of him. Not when God was in control. And no matter what happened, God would still be in control. "Because we can protect you."

Martin scoffed.

"It doesn't have to be like this," he repeated. "The police can search for this truck much more effectively, especially if it's out here in the middle of nowhere. We don't have to walk miles and miles."

It was cold, and the January wind whipped at his face. Soon enough they'd all have red cheeks and chapped lips. Not devastating, but so unnecessary.

Most of this could have been avoided. Patrick tried not to get angry, but it was there.

"These people don't have to threaten your life. We can get the drugs off the streets. We'll protect you, and maybe even try to talk the army into not putting you in prison for deserting your obligation and disappearing. If you testify against whomever you got the drugs from, we can make sure they stop. Cut off the drug trade and get more of those substances off the streets."

It was poison, and it killed every day while it sucked in yet more people to the tangled web of addiction. No one wanted that. But Martin, following in his father's footsteps, could be a whole other story. Maybe he didn't care. He was just out to make money.

"That's how you think you'll talk me down?" Martin asked. "Offer me a minimum wage life under a new name, some nobody in some nowhere town? Stop me from hurting any more people." Those last few words were said in a high, whiny voice.

Patrick bit down on his molars. "It's the right thing. After what you've done? I doubt you'll be free even a year before you die. And here you are, racking up even more charges. Digging your hole deeper." Anger got the better of him. "I hope you fall in it."

This guy was going straight to military prison when the army caught up and he finally had to explain what those incidents in Afghanistan were about. Patrick figured they had charges in the works and Martin had essentially slipped bail.

Then there were the civilian charges. He could've disappeared. Instead, he'd resurrected a legacy of crime and death just to make a buck.

Guys like him were the kind of people Tucker flushed out every day. People with no regard for others, only themselves.

Patrick leaned down and petted his dog's flank.

Tucker barked.

Patrick looked at him, then at the expanse of land in front of them. "What is it, buddy?"

He thought he saw something up ahead. Probably just a critter Tucker smelled, but he walked faster. Shrub brushes collected together, as though congregation was more important than height. A bundle of sand shinnery oak stood together. The dirt behind looked like it might be a path, or some kind of fire road.

Old. Abandoned.

"The truck!" Jennie moved to his left, staying out of Martin's arm reach. He didn't blame her for that.

They all circled the bushes and saw the truck, on its side. Patrick looked in the front windshield and said, "There's blood on the window."

The open door at the top was the passenger side. Was that how the dead man had climbed out? The driver's door was smashed against the dirt.

"I think he hit a rut and flipped over. Hit his head." And still managed to climb out and walk or crawl to where he now lay? That was some determination. Patrick almost admired the man.

"Check inside." Martin waved his gun from pointing to Patrick's torso to the truck.

"Secret compartment, like the old bootleg days?"

"Get in there."

Patrick walked to Jennie instead, leading Tucker. "Can you please hold the leash?"

The frown on her face indicated she was about as excited about this as he was. Patrick handed over the leash, then leaned down and quickly touched his lips to hers. He whispered, "It'll be okay."

She shot him a wry look, but it was soft.

Patrick went back to Martin. Before he climbed to the open door and got in, he wanted all the information. "Any guesses on where this stash is hidden?"

Martin clearly didn't want to answer but he said, "Under the floorboard behind the front seat."

Patrick looked at the sky and sighed. When he retrieved the drugs, would Martin simply shoot them and walk off with his stash? Patrick didn't like the idea that they would be left for dead out here. *I'll raise your son as my own.* The thought of that made him want to throw up as Jennie had done when confronted with the dead body.

"Let's go, cop."

Patrick pressed his lips in a thin line. "You don't have

to try bargaining with these guys. It can end differently… with you doing the right thing."

No more loss of life. No more threat.

"Your nephew doesn't need to be an orphan."

He heard Jennie's soft gasp but couldn't comfort her right now. Patrick needed to eliminate the threat here first. Otherwise it was all over.

Martin said, "As long as I'm alive, what do I care?"

"If that guy is hurting him—"

"Get in the truck and get my drugs." Martin pointed the gun at Patrick's face. He realized then that it was his gun.

"He's right," Jennie called out. "You don't have to do this." *To Nate.* She didn't say it, but he heard the words anyway. They made his chest hurt in a way it never had before. "It's not right. You're only causing more pain. Don't do this."

One final plea for her brother to do the right thing. But it fell on deaf ears. Or stubborn ones.

Martin shifted the gun from Patrick to her. His own sister.

Patrick realized what was about to happen. He moved, instinct firing his muscles. He ran for Jennie and Tucker, determined to protect them.

The gunshot cracked like a firework. Without thinking, Patrick tackled Jennie.

Pain shot through his shoulder as he fell toward her. Tucker yelped at them. Jennie screamed as the two of them hit the ground together.

TWENTY-ONE

It took Jennie a second to realize she was screaming. She sucked in a breath—which caused the noise to cease for a second—and blew it out the way she had when she'd birthed Nate. Everything that had just happened rushed back in one go.

Martin. Tucker. Patrick.

Focus.

"Patrick." She touched his shoulder with one hand, pushing at his weight, and pressed two fingers to his neck with the other. The man she loved. The one who had saved her life. "Rick…" Calling him that was so natural now, even if it was little more than a breathy moan. "Rick."

His weight was heavy on her, and she felt a steady pulse. Tucker barked. The wet feel of… *Don't think about that.* A buzzing noise interrupted her thoughts. Patrick still hadn't moved or even moaned. She turned his face to her and patted his cheek. "Wake up. Please wake up."

"Cops!" One of the gunmen beat feet away from them. Scurrying off to try to escape what was inevitable.

"No, they're army!" someone else shouted.

Whoever it was, Jenny didn't much care. Either way,

they were the good guys and she wanted these bad guys to leave. Or at least not try to hurt any of them again.

Tucker barked. He sounded agitated, and she realized she was learning his temperaments. Jennie looked at her brother, who had tried to kill her. Gun pointed, trigger pulled, actually *fired a shot* in her direction. She couldn't believe it. So much so that it wasn't just Patrick's weight causing her to be breathless.

Martin stared up at the sky, his jaw hard. His reckoning was coming. But not before he told them where Nate was. Still at Patrick's house, or somewhere else?

Jennie would get her son back. She would. *God, keep my son safe until I get there.*

Patrick groaned. Jennie rolled him off her, onto the ground beside her. Tucker leaned forward on his four paws. After a second of tension, he barked twice. The action caused his front paws to lift off the ground as he announced his displeasure at Martin.

"Tucker!"

She didn't want her brother to hurt him. What if Tucker got injured and Patrick wasn't conscious enough to intervene?

Patrick groaned again and she heard him suck in a long breath. The next sound from him was a moan.

Jennie didn't know if it would work, but she said, "Tucker, come!" using a loud, commanding voice like Patrick did.

The dog glanced at her.

"Come."

He started toward her.

Jennie peeled off her sweater. When she turned back to Patrick, she tried not to react. Tried. A whimper escaped her lips. She balled up the fabric and pressed it hard against his shoulder, leaning on him with as much weight as she could.

He moaned again, his eyes focused on her.

"You were shot. Don't move." Jennie looked at the sky. A helicopter? Whether it was the army or the state police, she didn't care. "Help is on the way. Just hang tight, okay?"

Most of the gunmen had fled.

She looked around for her brother and saw him climb the side of the truck. Patrick had done it much more easily. It took Martin a couple of attempts before he managed to haul himself to the open door so he could drop inside.

Those moments Patrick had been beside the truck and she'd been by her brother and the other gunmen, even holding on to Tucker's leash, had been some of the scariest of her life. Now her brother was behind the windshield. Trying to get the drugs? She glanced at the helicopter. The authorities were closing in.

Soon there would be nowhere to go.

She turned back to Patrick. "Are you okay?"

He nodded. Jennie wasn't sure she believed him.

"You need to be okay." She held the sweater tight. Patrick lifted a hand and placed it over hers. She said, "You have to be here when I get Nate back."

"I…" He gasped a breath but didn't finish, pain washing over his face.

Her heart soared just at the idea that he still cared about her. There was no time for that to sink in, though. Not the full extent of what it would mean for them. For their son, and the future.

She leaned down and touched her lips to his in a fast kiss. "We'll talk later. When things are safe."

Her brother rooted around in the cab of the truck.

His men had disappeared. In the distance three big

Humvee-looking vehicles kicked up dust as they approached in formation. The helicopter was closer now, circling around them.

Those men would swarm over this whole area. Martin would be locked down.

She couldn't let him be taken by the authorities without telling her where that man had taken Nate.

She looked at Tucker. "Stay." Then she clambered to her feet. She stumbled but managed to stay standing. What should she do? Martin had dropped the gun before he climbed into the truck. She swiped the weapon from the ground and realized it was Patrick's. Jennie moved around to the windshield and planted her feet.

She raised the weapon and pointed it at the glass. "Martin!"

He looked up. A split second of fear crossed his face, and then he turned back to his search.

"Tell me where Nate is!"

He didn't respond. She said it a couple more times, but got no response.

Jennie redirected her aim to the bottom corner of the windshield, in front of the steering wheel. She squeezed the trigger and fired a shot.

Jerk. Exhale. She fixed her stance and readied to fire again. She took a long breath and let it out slowly. Calm. That was what Nate needed right now.

"Tell me!"

Her brother shifted. From behind the windshield she'd just shattered, he turned to face her. His first shot slammed a baseball-size hole through the windshield.

She yelped and jumped out of the way. He still had his gun.

The second shot was closer. Jennie dove for the ground. She saw him climb out the door, and she lifted her arm. Empty hand. Jennie looked around for the weapon.

As soon as she had it in her grasp and lifted it, he'd disappeared out of view. She ran to the truck and saw him beyond it, sprinting away at full speed, hauling a duffel bag over his shoulder.

Tucker's dog tags jingled.

He passed her, racing after her brother.

"Tucker!" Martin would surely shoot him. Right?

The helicopter circled in front of her brother. She heard a yell, but didn't know where it came from. As Jennie watched, the dog launched himself at her brother and took him to the ground.

A gunshot rang out.

"Tucker!"

Patrick gritted his teeth and rolled. He managed to get up and stumble toward Jennie as white spots floated across his vision. His teeth ached, he was clenching so hard.

He nearly went down but snatched the gun from her. She gasped.

Patrick moved to Martin and Tucker, giving his dog a quick pet.

Martin groaned. His legs shifted, but he couldn't get up with the weight of Tucker on his back. Patrick noticed a knot forming on Martin's forehead.

Patrick held out his hand to the dog. He had nothing to give Tucker, so he rubbed the sides of his face and put his own close. "Good boy."

His equilibrium shifted and Patrick nearly fell forward. Nausea rolled in his stomach and he had to admit his shoulder screamed fire right now. He pushed out a breath between his teeth and planted a knee.

He waved a hand for Tucker to back up. "Down."

The dog moved off Martin. Patrick stuck a knee in Jennie's brother's back.

A uniformed man approached. "Hands up!"

Patrick lifted one hand. "New Mexico State Police."

"You're Officer Sanders?"

He nodded. "She's with me."

Jennie flushed with relief. Even dirty and bedraggled, her expression full of fear and adrenaline, he thought she'd never looked more beautiful.

Standing around them was a crowd of uniformed state police, interspersed with a lot of camo-dressed army guys. Some had MP bands on their arms. All had high-powered rifles.

"We'll take that guy off your hands." The soldier held a hand out, and Patrick clasped his forearm. The guy practically hauled him off his feet—a sergeant. Ready to take Martin into custody. Finally. Well, Patrick was the one who had found him.

They weren't going to take Martin away until he told them where Nate was.

When he turned to see them cuff Martin and lift him up—a whole lot less gently—Patrick said, "Where is Nate?"

The army guys glanced at him. Patrick kept his focus on the man who would've been his brother-in-law. He even might still be now, after Patrick and Jennie figured everything out. And got their son back.

Patrick took a step. The movement sent pain through his torso. He was assuming there was no serious damage. He'd been shot in the shoulder and was pretty sure the bullet had gone all the way through—out the back. The best scenario. It wasn't naïve to think like that—it was hope.

He grunted. "Will that guy kill him?" Patrick needed to know.

Jennie sniffed back tears.

"He's your nephew, Martin. You turned him over to that guy? You want me to bring you up on more kidnapping and accessory charges on top of all the trouble you're already in?" He was personally involved in this case. Patrick wasn't going to be the one to pursue this, given the army was involved, but he would make sure the full force of the law came down on Martin Wilson's head.

"I want a deal. Then I'll tell you where he is."

Patrick got in his face. "No deal. You shot me, and you had your guy kidnap my son. Twice. Where is he?"

He wasn't going to threaten the man in front of this many people. That wouldn't go down well. Patrick would find it hard to support his family if he were fired—or thrown in jail himself.

But Martin knew what he implied.

"Where is he?"

Given the gunshot wound, Patrick couldn't fight him. Martin was cuffed anyway.

Maybe a few days ago he'd have wanted revenge. Before Patrick learned that trust in God was his best weapon.

Make him tell me.

It was an honest prayer, but maybe not theologically correct. Patrick needed all the help he could get right now.

"Sanders!"

He turned again and saw Eric running toward him. Behind Eric, Sheriff Johns walked a cuffed gunman toward their huddle. The sheriff had a wound on the side of his face, as though the guy had fought being cuffed and Johns had taken the man down. Eric had a smudge of dirt on the front of his shirt.

Patrick swayed, light-headed all of a sudden. Jennie lifted his arm on his good side and stood under it, holding him up.

Eric stopped in front of them.

"We need to find Nate."

Patrick was glad she'd said it. He wasn't sure he could put the words together right now.

"Your man needs a hospital." The army sergeant passed Martin off to one of his men and came over to Eric. He motioned to indicate Patrick and said, "You should take him in. We've got this covered, and the sheriff can round up Wilson's men."

"We need to find my son." Patrick forced the words out through gritted teeth. "Martin knows where he is."

"Martin says differently," the sergeant said. "Told me he doesn't know where his man took your boy."

"*His* nephew." Tucker leaned against his leg, but Patrick would probably pass out if he touched his dog's fur right now. That was the side where he'd been shot in his shoulder.

The sergeant nodded. "I'll keep working, but if he asks for a lawyer, there's nothing I can do. He won't get a deal. I'm sorry." He looked apologetic, even as he shrugged it off. "He's coming with me."

Eric waved a cell phone. "We found this on one of the gunmen. We can track every cell it communicated with in the last three days. Get all their GPS locations and figure out who isn't here. Maybe we can find Nate that way."

"That will take too long."

"We have all these guys—" Johns shifted the man he held "—so maybe one of them will talk."

The cuffed gunman laughed. "What's it worth? Cause I want a deal, too."

Patrick wanted to punch him. Not constructive, but it was how he felt.

Jennie straightened her shoulders. "Tell us where he is." She should have sounded distraught. Instead, she sounded strong...and full of grief. "Don't you have people you care about?" she asked the gunman. "How would you feel if one of them was in danger?"

The gunman's lips quirked, and he huffed.

"Can Tucker find him?"

Patrick squeezed his eyes shut as he thought it over through all the pain in his shoulder. "We need something to get a scent from, and we can start from the last place he was seen."

Eric pulled out his keys. "I'll drive."

Patrick opened his eyes and met his partner's gaze.

Eric said, "We'll find him."

He nodded. Patrick had no intention of stopping until he found Nate. He would probably keel over on the way, but he wouldn't back down.

They started for the car. Eric ran ahead and drove over the desert they'd walked, back to pick them up. They had no idea where Nate was. None of the gunmen had talked, and Martin either didn't know or refused to say. *I don't care.* It wouldn't stop them from finding him.

Eric drove to the rental house and went inside with Jennie to get a shirt, or something Tucker could pick up a scent from. Patrick shifted in his seat to face Tucker, in the back of Eric's SUV. "Hey, buddy."

Tucker sniffed Patrick's face, then licked his cheek. Normally that wasn't okay—because it was gross—but Patrick realized a tear had rolled down. Better that it was gone when Jennie came back.

"You wanna find Nate?"

The dog whined. Probably just a reaction to the tone of

Patrick's voice—a brokenness and fear he'd never heard from his handler before.

Jennie brought a shirt back, and Eric drove them to Patrick's old house. He couldn't think about the past. This was about Nate, not his own feelings.

Eric pulled up behind the house.

Patrick had Tucker scent the shirt. "Is that Nate?" The dog took a big sniff, reacting in a way he never had before. Tucker knew who wasn't there. "Are you ready, Tuck? Wanna go? Ready? Let's go!" The dog bounced up and down, tugging on the leash. "Tucker, find!"

The dog raced ahead of him. Patrick fought the pain and led the way, leading Jennie back to their son.

On the most important search of all their lives.

We're coming, Nate.

TWENTY-TWO

Jennie was exhausted. Tucker was the only one who didn't seem to be. The dog had energy for days. Patrick and his K-9 partner raced ahead. Eric came second, with Jennie behind him. She didn't even know how Patrick was still functioning.

He'd been shot. Her life with him had flashed before her eyes as she'd pressed her sweater into his wound.

Now he was walking around?

"You love him, don't you?"

She glanced over to find Eric watching her as they both trotted along, trying to keep up with Patrick. "Um… what?"

Her brain wasn't exactly firing on all cylinders right now. She watched Patrick ahead of them. Love him?

"I always have. Not much changed, even after he left town. As much as I wanted to hate him for leaving me alone, I never really did. And now I know what happened, and why, there's no animosity there at all."

This was good. They were racing across the desert behind Patrick's old house—actually heading in the direction of her house. The distraction of conversation helped her not think about how much her legs ached. She would collapse eventually. Hopefully not before they found Nate, because that would only slow down the search.

Eric eyed her. "He's a good man."

"I know that." She huffed out the words, breathy now that they'd been running for nearly fifteen minutes. "Probably the best man I know."

Patrick was better than anyone and everyone she'd ever met—except Nate. Father and son were tied on that scale.

God, help us find Nate.

"Because he's your son's father?"

She shot Eric a look. That's what Patrick's partner thought of her? Jennie only appreciated Patrick because of his biological connection to their son? If it was true, it was also completely shallow. She could separate the two.

If she only acknowledged him because of the fact he'd fathered Nate, that meant she saw no additional value in him.

Jennie would never shortchange Patrick like that. He had so much honor and worth. His mom had raised a good man, regardless of how she'd felt about Jennie. They could get to a place where Nate would have his grandmother in his life, and two parents that respected each other and loved him.

Underneath it all, Jennie would still feel that same pain she'd always carried. Knowing what she'd lost, because of her father. What she could never have back.

There was simply too much hurt between them. Her family had tried, at every opportunity, to destroy Patrick. Her love wasn't stronger than the pain he'd endured—or the grief over all he'd lost.

He would never forgive her.

She picked up speed, ready to get to her son. She'd

seen Tucker search a couple of times now. Given how he was acting, he clearly had something. *Nate.*

Despite how sweet Patrick had been, this was about him and Nate. About bringing a grandmother into her son's life. And having the chance for him to get to know his father. They'd slipped back into old habits on a few occasions, with those wonderful hugs. The times he'd kissed her forehead.

But this wasn't about a relationship between them. And it never would be when she couldn't believe his feelings were real. Not just because she wanted Nate to have a true family. She'd never trust his affection had no strings.

"Is Patrick going to be okay?" Jennie asked.

"If he isn't, we're here for him anyway. Right?"

Jennie nodded.

She figured by now that Patrick couldn't hear their conversation. He'd have reacted—hopefully well—to something she had said. Or he was just focused. Concentrating, as she was, on praying for Nate with every step, despite being drawn into a conversation with his partner. That was probably Eric's attempt to distract *her.*

"Thank you." She glanced at him again. "For being here." She motioned in front of her, toward Patrick. "For both of us, and Nate."

If something happened to Patrick, Eric could continue. Jennie wouldn't know the first thing about going up against a dangerous gunman. Though, she had to admit she'd done pretty well when faced with her brother. But that was different.

She'd have said he couldn't possibly try to hurt her, but he had.

Jennie fought a sigh. Later, she would cry over the lack of love between her and the only sibling she had.

She recognized where they were headed. "That's my

house." Nate's house. "Do you think that's where they went?"

"We'll find out. And if he's not there," Eric said, "we'll move on and find him."

Jennie swiped at the tears on her cheeks and nodded.

Patrick turned. "We need to search the house." His face was pale. As she watched, he started to keel over.

Jennie ran to him and ducked under his good shoulder, as she had before. "I've got you."

"We need to get in there."

Eric said, "I'll go."

"Tucker can clear the house and find Nate."

"If the door was open." Eric shot him a knowing look. "I'll go inside and leave the door ajar. Once I'm out of sight, tell Tucker to come in. At least he'll be a distraction to the man holding Nate. At best, I can take the guy down and he can find Nate."

"You take the man." Patrick nodded. "Tucker will find Nate."

Relief rolled through her. The wash of it was like sunshine on a cold day. Sudden warmth and happiness. *Nate.* They were so close.

Was he really inside?

She couldn't even contemplate the worst that could have already happened. That didn't bear thinking about. Not when God had brought them this far.

You did, didn't You? Thank You.

There was one final hurdle, but she was grateful anyway.

"Copy that." Eric didn't waste any time. He raced over to the house, head low and gun drawn. Should they have called for backup? Maybe there was no time. Also, she didn't want the man holding Nate to freak out at multiple approaching cops and wind up hurting Nate in a way that none of them could recover from.

She shivered just thinking about it.

Eric kicked in the back door and moved inside. Patrick showed Tucker the shirt again, so he could get Nate's scent. "Tucker, find!"

She held her breath as the dog darted across the yard. "It'll be okay."

She nodded. "I know." More just to say the words aloud than because she believed them. "It has to be. I can't lose him the way I lost you."

His arm squeezed her. She reached up and took hold of his hand. Patrick turned his face so his mouth was against her cheek. "You didn't lose me."

Inside the house, a gunshot rang out.

Then another answering shot.

Jennie sucked in a breath. "Nate."

"Hold on."

Jennie's whole body shuddered. Patrick held her tight in his one good arm. "Just hold on."

He wanted to go inside the house and help Eric.

Right now he would be a liability, and Jennie had no way to defend herself. Tucker was in there, and Eric.

"Hold on." He said the words a third time, repeating the mantra as much to her as to himself as seconds ticked by like minutes and it felt like an hour before Tucker let out one short, sharp bark.

Where was Eric? Who had been shot? Patrick had more questions, but standing took a lot of brain power. It *hurt*.

They made their way to the house. He had to grit his teeth with each step, and he knew the dental bill alone after all this would be killer.

But if they got Nate back, it would also be worth it.

Eric appeared in the doorway, clutching his arm. "The gunman is dead."

"You got hit?"

"Just a scratch. Unlike you."

Patrick wasn't going to banter right now. "Tucker found Nate?"

Eric nodded and moved aside. Jennie let go of Patrick and he swayed. His partner led him to the hall and he collapsed against the wall. Probably bleeding on the drywall paint. Leaving a smudge. He tried to turn to see where Jennie had gone, but pain tore through him and he hissed out a breath.

Where was Tucker?

And where was Nate? It had been hours. He wanted his son back.

"I'll step out and call this in," Eric said. When Patrick glanced over, he added, "Dead guy is in the dining room."

"Copy—" Bile rose and he couldn't get any more words out.

"You need an ambulance."

He needed his son.

"Nate!" Jennie called out to the boy. It sounded like she was running through the house. Frantic. Searching. Was he hiding? Had that man told him to duck inside some closet and stay there?

Patrick turned the other direction and saw Tucker sitting by the kitchen at a door. Waiting for him? No. He'd found Nate, right? "Tuck."

The dog barked. His body moved the way it did when his tail wagged. But he stayed in that "Sit" and he didn't break it.

Nate was there.

Patrick tried to push off the wall, but he couldn't control his weight and started to keel over. He slammed into the other wall and cried out, "Jennie, he's in here!"

He heard her coming. Down the hall. The patter of her feet closing in. "Tucker." He breathed out his dog's name.

Patrick couldn't move. Pain sparked tears in his eyes. He needed to get to his son. Given all the blood, he was going to scare the boy witless the second Nate saw him. He frowned, gasped a breath and tried not to lose it as Jennie raced past him.

"Laundry room."

She didn't even pause, just sprinted to the door and petted Tucker. Then told him to get out of the way.

Patrick heard the shuffle, pushed along the wall and looked around the corner.

He managed a couple of steps. His dog sniffed his hand, but Patrick didn't have the strength to even pat his head.

He made it to the table, braced his weight and kept going to the kitchen counter. He grabbed the dish towel hanging on the oven and pressed the towel against his wound. The pain made him want to throw up, fall down or pass out. Perhaps all three. He settled for sliding down the wall.

Jennie opened the door. Nate was huddled in the corner where Patrick could see he had no visible injuries but looked seriously pale. She crouched. "Hey." Nate's gaze shifted from her to Patrick. Jennie touched Nate's shoulder. "You okay?"

Nate said nothing. His cheeks were red over the pale color. Patrick couldn't tell if they were flushed from fear and crying or if he'd been slapped around. Told to stay where he was. Scared enough he couldn't move now.

Patrick swallowed down nausea the pain was causing. "Hey, buddy."

Nate's gaze shifted to him again.

"I hurt my arm." There was a whole room between them, but he kept his voice low. "Will you go see the doctor with me?"

Nate looked at his mom, then back at Patrick. He chewed his lip. "He told me not to move."

"He's gone now." Jennie touched Nate's cheeks. "That man is not going to hurt you anymore."

Tucker wandered in and stopped by Patrick's boot. He motioned with a flick of his fingers. "Go."

The dog trotted to Nate and licked the boy in the face. Nate squealed and giggled. It was subdued, but it was there. "Hi, Tucker."

The dog sniffed his son's neck and then lay down by his side. He put his paw on Nate's lap. Not something Patrick normally allowed, asking for affection like that. But this time he let it go. Clearly the two of them had something special, and right now it seemed like it was more important for Nate to feel safe than anything else Patrick might have to correct in the ornery Airedale's training later.

Eric came in. "Ambulance will be here in five."

Patrick tried to nod. His consciousness faded toward black, but he fought it for every inch of hold it wanted to take. "Thanks."

Jennie shifted. He heard her pet his dog, his good boy and the best dog ever. *Yes, you are.* Then Patrick felt warm fingers touch his cheeks. "Hey there. Hang on, okay?"

He tried to focus on her face. Couldn't make his eyes do what they were supposed to. "Love you." He needed her to know. No matter what, he'd always loved her.

And he always would.

* * *

"Is Dad okay?"

Jennie held steady to Nate's hand, clutched in hers. "The doctors just need to make sure. But they said he's awake, right? So that's good."

He'd told her he loved her.

Jennie wanted to curl up and cry. It just hurt more, knowing neither of their feelings had ever changed. But that still didn't mean he forgave her for what her family had done to him.

Or for putting their son in danger.

Jennie led Nate down the hall to Patrick's hospital room. At the door she said, "Do you want me to go first?"

If Patrick was bandaged and hooked to machines, it could be scary.

Nate shook his head and didn't let go of her hand. He'd stuck with her as much as possible in the last day or so since they'd found him at home. She didn't blame him. Jennie wasn't feeling much like being separated from her son right now. Later they would need to work through those feelings. Right now they were just enjoying the closeness of having each other back.

Jennie held the door open.

"Hey, guys." Eric pushed off the wall, an easy smile on his face. "Good timing. I should be going." He ruffled Nate's hair and hurried out.

"What was that about?"

Patrick grinned. It was strained, but there. "He has a date with your friend Beth."

Jennie turned to the door then back. Patrick laughed, and Nate leaned against her hip while his father groaned. "Ouch. That does not feel good." He smiled down at their son. "Hey, buddy. Have you been taking care of Tucker?"

Nate nodded.

Jennie moved forward with him, close enough Patrick could hold out his hand and Nate could lean in for a gentle hug.

"I'm okay."

"Me, too," Nate said. "We stayed at the rental house last night. They have DVDs."

"Anything good?"

Nate shrugged. "Will you be out soon?"

Jennie nearly smiled. It sounded like Patrick was in jail, not in the hospital. Patrick returned her smile. "I hope so." His brow furrowed. "Do you think maybe… when I am, you might want to come home with me and see my house?"

Jennie's stomach hardened. She opened her mouth to say something, but no words came out. What was she supposed to say?

"You and your mom could stay in my guest room, and you could see where Tucker lives."

That sounded nice but didn't exactly answer the questions rolling through her mind.

Patrick glanced at her, some of those questions on his face. She still wasn't sure what she should say.

Nate answered for her. "That could be good." He looked at her.

She nodded. "I like it." For her son, she could do anything.

Nate smiled. The first time since being kidnapped. He wandered to the chair and plopped onto the seat, slouching down.

She was about to pass him his backpack, so he had something to do, when she felt Patrick's warm fingers touch hers.

She let her gaze slide to him.

"Yeah?"

Jennie nodded. He tugged her closer. Enough she got the message and leaned in.

"Ella tried to kiss me at recess," Nate said. "I didn't let her because it's gross."

Patrick's eyes flashed with a smile. Jennie tried to smile back, but it wavered. Patrick whispered, "You know how I feel. How I've always felt."

She shook her head. "After everything my family has done to you?"

He studied her face. "I'm thinking since your father and brother haven't been in your life for a long time, maybe ever, that makes me and Nate your real family."

He really thought that? Tears filled her eyes. "I got you shot."

"Jennie, you didn't hurt me. I'm guessing this—" he wiped the tears from her cheeks "—is because you actually love me."

"I never stopped." She grasped his wrists, determined to hold on tight and never let go. "I've always loved you, and I always will."

"Good." Patrick tugged her to him and kissed her. "You're the one for me. I knew it in high school, but I know it even more now. I want us to be together. For real."

Jennie nodded. "Me, too."

"Marriage, Jennie. We need to give Nate a real family." Patrick kissed her again. "The family neither of us had."

"Do you really think we can do this?"

"Yes." He sounded so sure. "If we do it together."

Jennie's heart soared. She had everything she'd ever longed for, right here.

EPILOGUE

One Year Later

"Go, Nate!" Jennie jumped up and down, but it was short lived given how exhausted she felt. She watched her son from the sidelines as he ran with the ball, avoiding all the other kids on the opposing team trying to snatch his flag.

"Run! Run!" Beside Jennie, Patrick's mother cheered, also. Then she turned to Jennie and they shared a smile.

It had taken some time, but the two of them had rebuilt trust, and now Nate's grandma was a huge part of his life. Mostly trying to balance being the "fun" grandma to make up for everything she'd missed and not letting things get out of control. Too many snacks wasn't good for anyone. But Jennie was enjoying watching them figure it out as they got to know each other.

As for the letters Patrick had written, Jennie figured her father had thrown them away. However, there was no way to ever know. So she'd let that go. Along with the rest of the hurt.

She sat on the blanket, letting out a satisfied sigh. The ring set fit snug on her left hand. Patrick had slid it there nearly two months ago now. Longer than either of them had wanted to wait, but it was for the best and gave them all time to adjust. They were different people now than they had been, building a relationship with God and with each other.

They were a family for real, both Jennie and Nate having the last name Sanders. Nothing of who she had been was a part of their lives now. How could it be, when that life had been loneliness and dishonesty and this one was filled with life and blessing?

Jennie lay back on the blanket and closed her eyes, overwhelmed to the point of exhaustion. Well, that wasn't the only reason.

Thank You, Lord.

So many blessings.

She woke to a strange sensation. As soon as she opened her eyes, she realized what it was. "Tucker. I told you how I feel about you licking my face." She shoved the dog away playfully and sat up.

Patrick crouched by her, dressed in his state police uniform. "I brought sandwiches."

She was about to thank him when pandemonium erupted on the flag football field. Barely seconds later Tucker had stolen some kid's flag and made a run for it while all the players and the coaches chased him. Nate fell on the ground, laughing.

Patrick sat by her, tugging her to his side. "You were asleep when I got here. Tired?"

She didn't like the worry on his face. "Yes, but it's not bad."

"What…?" He didn't finish.

Jennie leaned in, touched both his cheeks and spoke close. "I'm pregnant."

Cheers and congratulations erupted along with laughter on the blanket. And not just from his mother.

* * * * *

Dear Reader,

What a journey this has been. It reminds me of the promise God gives us, to bring beauty out of ashes. And doesn't He do that? What a blessing that we can live in the security of that promise. Whether it will happen on earth, or in Heaven, there is joy and blessing coming.

I pray this story has blessed you, and that you seek Him as you journey on.

I would love to hear from you by email through my website *www.authorlisaphillips.com* where you can fill out the contact form, and subscribe for news about new releases. I very much enjoy connecting with readers.

In Him,
Lisa Phillips